Juliana Horatia Gatty Ewing

Melchior's Dream : and other Tales

Juliana Horatia Gatty Ewing

Melchior's Dream : and other Tales

ISBN/EAN: 9783337024925

Printed in Europe, USA, Canada, Australia, Japan

Cover: Foto ©Andreas Hilbeck / pixelio.de

More available books at **www.hansebooks.com**

MELCHIOR'S DREAM

AND OTHER TALES.

By J. H. G.

EDITED BY MRS. ALFRED GATTY,

AUTHOR OF 'PARABLES FROM NATURE,' ETC.

ILLUSTRATED BY M. S. G.

LONDON:

BELL AND DALDY, 186, FLEET STREET.

1862.

Dedicated

TO

FOUR BROTHERS AND THREE SISTERS.

CONTENTS.

EDITOR'S PREFACE.

IT is always a memorable era in a mother's life when she first introduces a daughter into society. Many things contribute to make it so; among which is the fact of the personal blessing to herself, in having been permitted to see the day;—to have been spared, that is, to watch over her child in infancy, and now to see her entering life upon her own account.

But a more uncommon privilege is the one granted to me on the present occasion, of introducing a daughter into the literary world; and the feelings of pride and pleasure it calls forth, are certainly not less powerful than those created by the commoner occurrence. It

MELCHIOR'S DREAM.

AN ALLEGORY.

——◆——

"Thou that hast given so much to me,
Give one thing more—a grateful heart."
GEORGE HERBERT.

"WELL, Father, I don't believe the Browns are a bit better off than we are; and yet when I spent the day with young Brown, we cooked all sorts of messes in the afternoon; and he wasted twice as much rum and brandy and lemons in his trash, as I should want to make good punch of. He was quite surprised, too, when I told him that our mince-pies were kept shut up in the larder, and only brought out at meal-time, and then just one apiece; he said they had mince-pies always going, and he got one whenever he liked. Old Brown never blows up about that sort of thing; he likes Adolphus to enjoy himself in the holidays, particularly at Christmas."

B

The speaker was a boy—if I may be allowed to use the word in speaking of an individual whose jackets had for some time past been resigned to a younger member of his family, and who daily, in the privacy of his own apartment, examined his soft cheeks by the aid of his sisters' "back-hair glass." He was a handsome boy too; tall, and like David—"ruddy, and of a fair countenance;" and his face, though clouded then, bore the expression of general amiability. He was the eldest son in a large young family, and was being educated at one of the best public schools. He did not, it must be confessed, think either small beer or small beans of himself; and as to the beer and beans that his family thought of him, I think it was pale ale and kidney-beans at least.

Young Hopeful had, however, his weak points like the rest of us; and perhaps one of the weakest was the difficulty he found in amusing himself without *bothering* other people. He had quite a monomania for proposing the most troublesome "larks" at the most inconvenient moments; and if his plans were thwarted, an Æolian harp is cheerful compared to the tone in which, arguing and lamenting, he

"Fought his battles o'er again,"

to the distraction of every occupied member of the household.

When the lords of the creation of all ages can find nothing else to do, they generally take to eating and drinking; and so it came to pass that our hero had set his mind upon brewing a jorum of punch, and sipping it with an accompaniment of mince-pies; and Paterfamilias had not been quietly settled to his writing for half an hour, when he was disturbed by an application for the necessary ingredients. These he had refused, quietly explaining that he could not afford to waste his French brandy, etc., in school-boy cookery, and ending with, " You see the reason, my dear boy ?"

To which the dear boy replied as above, and concluded with the disrespectful (not to say ungrateful) hint, " Old Brown never blows up about that sort of thing; he likes Adolphus to enjoy himself in the holidays."

Whereupon Paterfamilias made answer, in the mildly deprecating tone in which the elder sometimes do answer the younger in these topsy-turvy days :—

" That's quite a different case. Don't you see, my boy, that Adolphus Brown is an only son, and you have nine brothers and sisters ?

If you have punch and mince-meat to play
with, there is no reason why Tom should not
have it, and James, and Edward, and William,
and Benjamin, and Jack.   And then there are
your sisters.   Twice the amount of the Browns'
mince-meat would not serve you.   I like you
to enjoy yourself in the holidays as much as
young Brown or anybody; but you must remember that I send you boys to good schools,
and give you all the substantial comforts and
advantages in my power; and the Christmas
bills are very heavy, and I have a great many
calls on my purse ; and you must be reasonable.
Don't you see?"

"Well, Father—" began the boy; but his
father interrupted him.   He knew the unvary-
ing beginning of a long grumble, and dreading
the argument, cut it short.

"I have decided.   You must amuse yourself
some other way.   And just remember that young
Brown's is quite another case.   He is an only
son."

Whereupon Paterfamilias went off to his study
and his sermon; and his son, like the Princess
in Andersen's story of the swineherd, was left
outside to sing,

> "O dearest Augustine,
> All's clean gone away!"

Not that he did say that—that was the princess's song ; what he said was,

"*I wish I was an only son !* "

This was rather a vain wish, for round the dining-room fire (where he soon joined them) were gathered his nine brothers and sisters, who, to say the truth, were not looking much more lively and cheerful than he. And yet (of all days in the year on which to be doleful and dissatisfied !) this was Christmas Eve.

Now I know that the idea of dullness or discomfort at Christmas is a very improper one, particularly in a story. We all know how every little boy in a story-book spends the Christmas holidays.

First, there is the large hamper of good things sent by grandpapa, which is as inexhaustible as Fortunatus's purse, and contains everything, from a Norfolk turkey, to grapes from the grandpaternal vinery.

There is the friend who gives a guinea to each member of the family, and sees who will spend it best.

There are the godpapas and godmammas, who might almost be fairy sponsors from the number of expensive gifts that they bring upon the scene. The uncles and aunts are also liberal.

One night is devoted to a magic-lautern (which has a perfect focus), another to the pantomime, a third to a celebrated conjuror, a fourth to a Christmas tree and juvenile ball.

The happy youth makes himself sufficiently ill with plum-pudding, to testify to the reader how good it was, and how much there was of it; but recovers in time to fall a victim to the negus and trifle at supper for the same reason. He is neither fatigued with late hours, nor surfeited with sweets; or if he is, we do not hear of it.

But as this is a strictly candid history, I will at once confess the truth, on behalf of my hero and his brothers and sisters. They had spent the morning in decorating the old church, in pricking holly about the house, and in making a misletoe bush. Then in the afternoon they had tasted the Christmas soup, and seen it given out; they had put a finishing touch to the snow man by crowning him with holly, and had dragged the yule-logs home from the carpenter's. And now, the early tea being over, Paterfamilias had gone to finish his sermon for to-morrow; his friend was shut up in his room; and Materfamilias was in hers, with one of those weary head-aches which even Christmas will not always keep away. So the ten juveniles were left to amuse themselves, and they found it rather a difficult matter.

"Here's a nice Christmas!" said our hero. He had turned his youngest brother out of the arm-chair, and was now lying in it with his legs over the side. "Here's a nice Christmas! A fellow might just as well be at school. I wonder what Adolphus Brown would think of being cooped up with a lot of children like this! It's his party to-night, and he's to have champagne and ices. I wish I was an only son."

"Thank you," said a chorus of voices from the floor. They were all sprawling about on the hearth-rug, pushing and struggling like so many kittens in a sack, and every now and then with a grumbled remonstrance :—

"Don't, Jack! you're treading on me."

"You needn't take all the fire, Tom."

"Keep your legs to yourself, Benjamin."

"It wasn't I," etc., with occasionally the feebler cry of a small sister—

"Oh! you boys are so rough."

"And what are you girls, I wonder?" inquired the proprietor of the arm-chair with cutting irony. "Whiney piney, whiney piney.

I wish there were no such things as brothers and sisters!"

"*You wish* WHAT?" said a voice from the shadow by the door, as deep and impressive as that of the ghost in Hamlet.

The ten sprang up; but when the figure came into the firelight, they saw that it was no ghost, but Paterfamilias's old college friend, who spent most of his time abroad, and who, having no home or relatives of his own, had come to spend Christmas at his friend's vicarage. "You wish *what?*" he repeated.

"Well, brothers and sisters are a bore," was the reply. "One or two would be all very well; but just look, here are ten of us; and it just spoils everything. If a fellow wants to go anywhere, it's somebody's else's *turn*. If old Brown sends a basket of grapes, it's share and share alike; all the ten must taste, and then there's about a grape and a half for each. If anybody calls or comes to luncheon, there are a whole lot of brats swarming about, looking as if we kept a school. Whatever one does, the rest must do; whatever there is, the rest must share; whereas, if a fellow was an only son, he would have the whole—and by all the rules of arithmetic, one is better than a tenth."

" And by the same rules, ten is better than one," said the friend.

"Sold again!" sang out Master Jack from the floor, and went head over heels against the fender.

His brother boxed his ears with great promptitude; and went on—"Well, I don't care; confess, Sir; isn't it rather a nuisance?"

Paterfamilias's friend looked very grave, and said quietly, "I don't think I am able to judge. I never had brother or sister but one, and he was drowned at sea. Whatever I have had, I have had the whole of, and would have given it away willingly for some one to give it to. If any one sent me grapes, I ate them alone. If I made anything, there was no one to show it to. If I wanted to act, I must act all the characters, and be my own audience. I remember that I got a lot of sticks at last, and cut heads and faces to all of them, and carved names on their sides, and called them my brothers and sisters. If you want to know what I thought a nice number for a fellow to have, I can only say that I remember carving twenty-five. I used to stick them in the ground and talk to them. I have been only, and lonely, and alone, all my life, and have never felt the nuisance you speak of."

This was a funny account; but the speaker looked so far from funny, that one of the sisters, who was very tender-hearted, crept up to him, and said gently—

"Richard is only joking; he doesn't really want to get rid of us. The other day the curate said he wished he had a sister, and Richard offered to sell us all for ninepence; but he is only in fun. Only it is rather slow just now, and the boys get rather cross; at least, we all of us do."

"It's a dreadful state of things," said the friend, smiling through his black beard and moustachios; "what is to be done?"

"I know what would be very nice," insinuated the young lady.

"What?"

"If you wouldn't mind telling us a very short story till supper-time. The boys like stories."

"That's a good un!" said Benjamin. "As if the girls didn't!"

But the friend proclaimed order, and seated himself with the girl in question on his knee. "Well, what sort of a story is it to be?"

"Any sort," said Richard; "only not too true, if you please. I don't like stories like tracts. There was an usher at a school I was

at, and he used to read tracts about good boys
and bad boys to the fellows on Sunday afternoon. He always took out the real names, and
put in the names of the fellows instead. Those
who had done well in the week, he put in as
good ones, and those who hadn't as the bad.
He didn't like me, and I was always put in
as a bad boy, and I came to so many untimely
ends, I got sick of it. I was hanged twice, and
transported once for sheep stealing; I committed suicide one week, and broke into the
bank the next; I ruined three families, became a
hopeless drunkard, and broke the hearts of my
twelve distinct parents. I used to beg him to let
me be reformed next week; but he said he never
would till I did my Cæsar better. So, if you
please, we'll have a story that can't be true."

"Very well," said the friend, laughing; "but
if it isn't true, may I put you in? All the best
writers, you know, draw their characters from
their friends nowadays. May I put you in?"

"Oh, certainly!" said Richard, placing himself in front of the fire, putting his feet on the
hob, and stroking his curls with an air which
seemed to imply that whatever he was put into
would be highly favoured.

The rest struggled, and pushed, and squeezed

themselves into more modest but equally comfortable quarters; and after a few moments of thought, Paterfamilias's friend commenced the story of

MELCHIOR'S DREAM.

"Melchior is my hero. He was—well, he considered himself a young man, so we will consider him so too. He was not perfect; but in these days the taste in heroes is for a good deal of imperfection, not to say wickedness. He was not an only son. On the contrary, he had a great many brothers and sisters, and found them quite as objectionable as my friend Richard does."

"I smell a moral," murmured the said Richard.

"Your scent must be keen," said the storyteller, "for it is a long way off. Well, he had never felt them so objectionable as on one particular night, when the house being full of company, it was decided that the boys should sleep in 'barracks,' as they called it; that is, all in one large room."

"Thank goodness we have not come to that!" said the incorrigible Richard; but he was reduced to order by threats of being turned out, and contented himself with burning the soles of his boots against the bars of the grate in silence : and the friend continued :—

" But this was not the worst. Not only was he, Melchior, to sleep in the same room with his brothers, but his bed being the longest and largest, his youngest brother was to sleep at the other end of it—foot to foot. True, by this means he got another pillow, for of course that little Hop-o'-my-thumb could do without one, and so he took his; but in spite of this, he determined that, sooner than submit to such an indignity, he would sit up all night. Accordingly, when all the rest were fast asleep, Melchior, with his boots off and his waistcoat easily unbuttoned, sat over the fire in the long lumber-room, which served that night as ' barracks.' He had refused to eat any supper downstairs to mark his displeasure, and now repaid himself by a stolen meal according to his own taste. He had got a pork-pie, a little bread and cheese, some large onions to roast, a couple of raw apples, an orange, and papers of soda and tartaric acid to compound effervescing draughts. When these dainties were finished, he proceeded to warm some beer in a pan, with ginger, spice, and sugar, and then lay back in his chair and sipped it slowly, gazing before him, and thinking over his misfortunes.

" The night wore on, the fire got lower and

lower; and still Melchior sat, with his eyes fixed
on a dirty old print, that had hung above the
mantelpiece for years, sipping his 'brew,' which
was fast getting cold.   The print represented an
old man in a light costume, with a scythe in one
hand, and an hour-glass in the other; and underneath the picture in flourishing capitals was
the word TIME.

"' You're a nice old beggar,' said Melchior
dreamily. 'You look like an old haymaker,
who has come to work in his shirt-sleeves, and
forgotten his bags!   Time! time you went to
the tailor's, I think.'

"This was very irreverent; but Melchior was
not in a respectful mood; and as for the old
man, he was as calm as any philosopher.

"The night wore on, and the fire got lower
and lower, and at last went out altogether.

"' How stupid of me not to have mended it !'
said Melchior; but he had not mended it, and
so there was nothing for it but to go to bed; and
to bed he went accordingly.

"' But I won't go to sleep,' he said; 'no,
no; I shall keep awake, and to-morrow they shall
know that I have had a bad night.'

"So he lay in bed with his eyes wide open,
and staring still at the old print, which he could

see from his bed by the light of the candle, which he had left alight on the mantelpiece to keep him awake. The flame waved up and down, for the room was draughty; and as the lights and shadows passed over the old man's face, Melchior almost fancied that it nodded to him, so he nodded back again; and as that tired him he shut his eyes for a few seconds. When he opened them again there was no longer any doubt—the old man's head was moving; and not only his head, but his legs, and his whole body. Finally, he put his feet out of the frame, and prepared to step right over the mantelpiece, candle, and all.

"'Take care,' Melchior tried to say, 'you'll set fire to your shirt.' But he could not utter a sound; and the old man arrived safely on the floor, where he seemed to grow larger and larger, till he was fully the size of a man, but still with the same scythe and hour-glass, and the same airy costume. Then he came across the room, and sat down by Melchior's bedside.

"'Who are you?' said Melchior, feeling rather creepy.

"'TIME,' said his visitor in a deep voice, which sounded as if it came from a distance.

"'Oh, to be sure, yes! In copper-plate capitals.'

" 'What's in copper-plate capitals?' inquired Time.

" 'Your name, under the print.'

" 'Very likely,' said Time.

" Melchior felt more and more uneasy. 'You must be very cold,' he said. 'Perhaps you would feel warmer if you went back into the picture.'

" 'Not at all,' said Time; 'I have come on purpose to see you.'

" 'I have not the pleasure of knowing you,' said Melchior, trying to keep his teeth from chattering.

" 'There are not many people who have a personal acquaintance with me,' said his visitor. 'You have an advantage—I am your godfather.'

" 'Indeed,' said Melchior; 'I never heard of it.'

" 'Yes,' said his visitor; 'and you will find it a great advantage.'

" 'Would you like to put on my coat?' said Melchior, trying to be civil.

" 'No, thank you,' was the answer. 'You will want it yourself. We must be driving soon.'

" 'Driving!' said Melchior.

" 'Yes,' was the answer; 'all the world is driving; and you must drive; and here come your brothers and sisters.'

" Melchior sat up ; and there they were, sure enough, all dressed, and climbing one after the other on to the bed—*his* bed !

" There was that little minx of a sister with her curls, (he always called them carrot shavings,) who was so conceited, (girls always are !) and always trying to attract notice, in spite of Melchior's incessant snubbings. There was that clever brother, with his untidy hair and bent shoulders, who was just as bad the other way ; who always ran out at the back door when visitors called, and was for ever moping and reading : and this, in spite of Melchior's hiding his books, and continually telling him that he was a disgrace to the family, a perfect bear, not fit to be seen, etc.,—all with the laudable desire of his improvement. There was that little Hop-o'-my-thumb, as lively as any of them, a young monkey, the worst of all ; who was always in mischief, and consorting with the low boys in the village ; though Melchior did not fail to tell him that he was not fit company for gentlemen's sons, that he was certain to be cut when he went to school, and that he would probably end his days by being transported, if not hanged. There was the second brother, who was Melchior's chief companion, and against

c

whom he had no particular quarrel. And there was the little pale lame sister, whom he dearly loved; but whom, odd to say, he never tried to improve at all; his remedy for her failings was generally, 'Let her do as she likes, will you?' There were others who were all tiresome in their respective ways; and one after the other they climbed up.

"'What are you doing, getting on to my bed!' inquired the indignant brother, as soon as he could speak.

"'Don't you know the difference between a bed and a coach, godson?' said Time sharply.

"Melchior was about to retort, but on looking round, he saw that they were really in a large sort of coach with very wide windows. 'I thought I was in bed,' he muttered. 'What can I have been dreaming of?'

"'What indeed!' said the godfather. 'But be quick, and sit close, for you have all to get in; you are all brothers and sisters.'

"'Must families be together?' inquired Melchior dolefully.

"'Yes, at first,' was the answer; 'they get separated in time. In fact, every one has to cease driving sooner or later. I drop them on the road at different stages, according to my orders,' and he showed a bundle of papers in his hands; 'but as I favour you, I will tell you in confidence that I have to drop all your brothers and sisters before you. There, you four oldest sit on this side, you five others there, and the little one must stand or be nursed.'

"'Ugh!' said Melchior, 'the coach would be well enough if one was alone; but what a squeeze with all these brats! I say, go pretty quick, will you?'

"'I will,' said Time, 'if you wish it. But I warn that you cannot change your mind. If I go quicker for your sake, I shall never go slow again; if slower, I shall not again go quick; and I only favour you so far, because you are my godson. Here, take the check-string; when you want me, pull it, and speak through the tube. Now we're off.'

"Whereupon the old man mounted the box, and took the reins. He had no whip; but when he wanted to start, he shook the hour-glass, and off they went. Then Melchior saw that the road where they were driving was very broad, and so filled with vehicles of all kinds that he could not see the hedges. The noise and crowd and dust were very great; and to Melchior all seemed delightfully exciting. There was every

sort of conveyance, from the grandest coach to
the humblest donkey-cart; and they seemed to
have enough to do to escape being run over.
Among all the gay people there were many
whom he knew; and a very nice thing it seemed
to be to drive among all the grandees, and to
show his handsome face at the window, and bow
and smile to his acquaintance. Then it appeared
to be the fashion to wrap oneself in a tiger-skin
rug, and to look at life through an opera-glass,
and old Time had kindly put one of each into
the coach.

" But here again Melchior was much troubled
by his brothers and sisters. Just at the moment when he was wishing to look most fashionable and elegant, one or other of them would
pull away the rug, or drop the glass, or quarrel,
or romp, or do something that spoilt the effect.
In fact, one and all, they 'just spoilt everything;' and the more he scolded, the worse
they became. The 'minx' shook her curls,
and flirted through the window with a handsome but ill-tempered looking man on a fine
horse, who praised her ' golden locks,' as he called
them; and oddly enough, when Melchior said
the man was a lout, and that the locks in question were corkscrewy carrot shavings, she only

seemed to like the man and his compliments
the more. Meanwhile, the untidy brother pored
over his book, or if he came to the window, it
was only to ridicule the fine ladies and gentlemen, so Melchior sent him to Coventry. Then
Hop-o'-my-thumb had taken to make signs and
exchange jokes with some 'larking' low looking youths in a dog-cart; and when his brother
would have put him to 'sit still like a gentleman' at the bottom of the coach, he seemed
positively to prefer his low companions; and
the rest were little better.

"Poor Melchior! Surely there never was a
clearer case of a young gentleman's comfort destroyed, solely by other people's perverse determination to be happy in their own way, instead of
in his. Surely, no young gentleman ever knew
better that if his brothers and sisters would yield
to his wishes, they would not quarrel; or ever
more completely overlooked the fact, that if he
had yielded more to theirs the same happy result might have been attained. At last he lost
patience, and pulling the check-string, bade
Godfather Time drive as fast as he could.

"'For,' said he, 'there will never be any
peace while there are so many of us in the
coach; if a fellow had the rug and glass, and

indeed the coach to himself, he might drive and
bow and talk with the best of them; but as it
is, one might as well go about in a wild-beast
caravan.'

"Godfather Time frowned, but shook his
glass all the same, and away they went at a
famous pace.   All at once they came to a stop.

"'Now for it,' said Melchior; 'here goes
one at any rate.'

"Time called out the name of the second
brother over his shoulder; and the boy stood
up, and bade his brothers and sisters good-bye.

"'It is time that I began to push my way
into the world,' said he, and passed out of the
coach, and in among the crowd.

"'You have taken the only quiet boy,' said
Melchior to the godfather angrily.   'Drive fast
now, for pity's sake; and let us get rid of the
tiresome ones.'

"And fast enough they drove, and dropped
first one and then the other; but the sisters,
and the reading boy, and the youngest still remained.

"'What are you looking at?' said Melchior
to the lame sister.

"'At a strange figure in the crowd,' she answered.

" 'I see nothing,' said Melchior. But on looking again after a while, he did see a figure wrapped in a cloak, gliding in and out among the people, unnoticed, if not unseen.

" 'Who is it?' Melchior asked of the god-father.

" 'A friend of mine,' Time answered. 'His name is Death.'

" Melchior shuddered, more especially as the figure had now come up to the coach, and put its hand in through the window, on which, to his horror, the lame sister laid hers and smiled. At this moment the coach stopped.

" 'What are you doing?' shrieked Melchior. 'Drive on! drive on!'

" But even while he sprang up to seize the check-string the door had opened, the pale sister's face (a little paler now) had dropped upon the shoulder of the figure in the cloak, and he had carried her away; and Melchior stormed and raved in vain.

" 'To take her, and to leave the rest! Cruel! cruel!'

" In his rage and grief, he hardly knew it when the untidy brother was called, and putting his book under his arm, slipped out of the coach without looking to the right or left. Presently

the coach stopped again; and when Melchior
looked up the door was open, and at it was the
fine man on the fine horse, who was lifting the
sister on to the saddle before him. 'What fool's
game are you playing?' said Melchior angrily.
'I know that man.   He is both ill-tempered
and a bad character.'

"'You never told her so before,' muttered
young Hop-o'-my-thumb.

"'Hold your tongue,' said Melchior. 'I for-
bade her to talk to him, which was enough.'

"'I don't want to leave you; but he cares
for me, and you don't,' sobbed the sister; and
she was carried away.

"When she had gone, the youngest brother
slid down from his corner and came up to Melchior.

"'We are alone now, Brother,' he said; 'let
us be good friends.   May I sit on the front seat
with you, and have half the rug? I will be very
good and polite, and will have nothing more to
do with those fellows, if you will talk to me.'

"Now Melchior really rather liked the idea;
but as his brother seemed to be in a submissive
mood, he thought he would take the opportunity
of giving him a good lecture, and would then
graciously relent and forgive.   So he began by

asking him if he thought that he was fit company for him (Melchior), what he thought that
gentlefolks would say to a boy who had been
playing with such youths as young Hop-o'-my-
thumb had, and whether the said youths were
not low rascals? And when the boy refused to
say that they were, (for they had been kind to
him,) Melchior said that his tastes were evidently as low as ever, and even hinted at the
old transportation threat. This was too much ;
the boy went angrily back to his window corner,
and Melchior—like too many of us !—lost the
opportunity of making peace for the sake of
wagging his own tongue.

" ' But he will come round in a few minutes,'
he thought. A few minutes passed, however,
and there was no sign. A few minutes more,
and there was a noise, a shout ; Melchior looked
up, and saw that the boy had jumped through
the open window into the road, and had been
picked up by the men in the dog-cart, and was
gone.

" And so at last my hero was alone. At first
he enjoyed it very much. He shook out his
hair, wrapped himself in the rug, stared through
the opera-glass, and did the fine gentleman very
well indeed. But though every one allowed him

to be the finest young fellow on the road, yet
nobody seemed to care for the fact as much as
he did; they talked, and complimented, and
stared at him, but he got tired of it. For he
could not arrange his hair any better; he could
not dispose the rug more gracefully; or stare
more perseveringly through the glass; and if
he could, his friends could do nothing more than
they had done. In fact, he got tired of the
crowd, and found himself gazing through the
window, not to see his fine friends, but to try
and catch sight of his brothers and sisters.
Sometimes he saw the youngest brother, looking each time more wild and reckless; and
sometimes the sister, looking more and more
miserable; but he saw no one else.

"At last there was a stir among the people,
and all heads were turned towards the distance,
as if looking for something. Melchior asked
what it was, and was told that the people were
looking for a man, the hero of many battles, who
had won honour for himself and for his country
in foreign lands, and who was coming home.
Everybody stood up and gazed, Melchior with
them. Then the crowd parted, and the hero
came on. No one asked whether he were
handsome or genteel, whether he kept good

company, or wore a tiger-skin rug, or looked
through an opera-glass? They knew what he
had *done*, and it was enough.

"He was a bronzed hairy man, with one sleeve
empty, and a breast covered with stars; but in
his face, brown with sun and wind, overgrown
with hair, and scarred with wounds, Melchior
saw his second brother! There was no doubt
of it. And the brother himself, though he
bowed kindly in answer to the greetings showered
on him, was gazing anxiously for the old coach,
where he used to ride and be so uncomfortable,
in that time to which he now looked back as the
happiest of his life.

"'I thank you, gentlemen. I am indebted to
you, gentlemen. I have been away long. I am
going home.'

"'Of course he is!' shouted Melchior, waving
his arms widely with pride and joy. 'He is
coming home; to this coach, where he was—
oh, it seems but an hour ago; Time goes so fast.
We were great friends when we were young together. My brother and I, ladies and gentlemen, the hero and I—my brother—the hero
with the stars upon his breast—he is coming
home!'

"Alas! what avail stars and ribbons on a

breast where the life-blood is trickling slowly
from a little wound ? The crowd looked anxious ;
the hero came on, but more slowly, with his dim
eyes straining for the old coach ; and Melchior
stood with his arms held out in silent agony.
But just when he was beginning to hope, and
the brothers seemed about to meet, a figure
passed between—a figure in a cloak.

"'I have seen you many times, friend, face
to face,' said the hero; 'but now I would
fain have waited for a little while.'

"'To enjoy his well-earned honours,' murmured the crowd.

"'Nay,' he said, 'not that; but to see my
home, and my brothers and sisters. But if it
may not be, friend Death, I am ready, and tired
too.' With that he held out his hand, and
Death lifted up the hero of many battles like a
child, and carried him away, stars and ribbons
and all.

"'Cruel Death !' cried Melchior ; 'was there
no one else in all this crowd, that you must
take him ?'

" His friends condoled with him ; but they
soon went on their own ways ; and the hero
seemed to be forgotten ; and Melchior, who had
lost all pleasure in the old bowings and chat-

tings, sat sadly gazing out of the window, to see if he could see any one for whom he cared. At last, in a grave dark man, who was sitting on a horse, and making a speech to the crowd, he recognized his clever untidy brother.

" ' What is that man talking about ?' he asked of some one near him.

"' That man !' was the answer. ' Don't you know ? He is *the* man of the time. He is a philosopher. Everybody goes to hear him. He has found out that—well—that everything is a mistake.'

" ' Has he corrected it ?' said Melchior.

" ' You had better hear for yourself,' said the man. ' Listen.'

" Melchior listened, and a cold clear voice rang upon his ear, saying :—

" ' The world of fools will go on as they have ever done; but to the wise few, to whom I address myself, I would say—Shake off at once and for ever the fancies and feelings, the creeds and customs that shackle you, and be true. We have come to a time when wise men will not be led blindfold in the footsteps of their predecessors, but will tear away the bandage, and see for themselves. I have torn away mine, and looked. There is no Faith—it is shaken to its rotten foundation; there is no Hope—it is disappointed every day; there is no Love at all. There is nothing for any man or for each, but his fate; and he is happiest and wisest who can meet it most unmoved.'

" 'It is a lie!' shouted Melchior. 'I feel it to be so in my heart. A wicked foolish lie! Oh! was it to teach such evil folly as this that you left home, and us, my brother? Oh, come back! come back!'

" The philosopher turned his head coldly, and smiled. ' I thank the gentleman who spoke,' he said, still in the same cold voice, 'for his bad opinion, and for his good wishes. I think the gentleman spoke of home and kindred. My experience of life has led me to find that home is most valued when it is left, and kindred most dear when they are parted. I have happily freed myself from such inconsistencies. I am glad to know that fate can tear me from no place that I care for more than the next where it shall deposit me, nor take away any friends that I value more than those it leaves. I re-commend a similar self-emancipation to the gentleman who did me the honour of speaking.'

"With this the philosopher went his way, and the crowd followed him.

" ' There is a separation more bitter than death,' said Melchior.

" At last he pulled the check-string, and called to Godfather Time in an humble entreating voice.

" ' It is not your fault,' he began ; ' it is not your fault, Godfather ; but this drive has been altogether wrong. Let us turn back, and begin again. Let us all get in afresh, and begin again.'

" ' But what a squeeze with all the brats !' said Godfather Time ironically.

" ' We should be so happy,' murmured Melchior humbly ; ' and it is very cold and chilly ; we should keep each other warm.'

" ' You have the tiger-skin rug and the opera-glass, you know,' said Time.

" ' Ah, do not speak of me !' cried Melchior earnestly. ' I am thinking of them. There is plenty of room ; the little one can sit on my knee ; and we shall be so happy. The truth is, Godfather, that I have been wrong. I have gone the wrong way to work. A little more love, and kindness, and forbearance, might have kept my sisters with us, might have led the little one to better tastes and pleasures, and have taught the other by experience the truth of the faith

and hope and love which he now reviles. Oh, I
have sinned! I have sinned! Let us turn back,
Godfather Time, and begin again. And oh!
drive very slowly, for partings come only too
soon.'

" 'I am sorry,' said the old man in the same
bitter tone as before, 'to disappoint your rather
unreasonable wishes. What you say is admirably
true, with this misfortune, that your good inten-
tions are too late. Like the rest of the world,
you are ready to seize the opportunity when it is
past. You should have been kind *then*. You
should have advised *then*. You should have
yielded *then*. You should have loved your
brothers and sisters while you had them. It is
too late now.'

"With this he drove on, and spoke no more,
and poor Melchior stared sadly out of the window. As he was gazing at the crowd, he suddenly saw the dog-cart, in which were his brother
and his wretched companions. Oh, how old and
worn he looked! and how ragged his clothes
were! The men seemed to be trying to persuade
him to do something that he did not like, and
they began to quarrel; but in the midst of the
dispute he turned his head, and caught sight of
the old coach; and Melchior seeing this, waved

his hands, and beckoned with all his might. The brother seemed doubtful; but Melchior waved harder, and (was it fancy?) Time seemed to go slower. The brother made up his mind; he turned and jumped from the dog-cart as he had jumped from the old coach long ago, and ducking in and out among the horses and carriages, ran for his life. The men came after him; but he ran like the wind—pant, pant, nearer, nearer; at last the coach was reached, and Melchior seized the prodigal by his rags and dragged him in.

"'Oh, thank God, I have got you safe, my brother!'

"But what a brother! with wasted body and sunken eyes! with the old curly hair turned to matted locks, that clung faster to his face than the rags did to his trembling limbs; what a sight for the opera-glasses of the crowd! What a subject for the tongues that were ever wagging, and complimenting, and backbiting, and lying, all in a breath, and without sense or scruple! What a sight and a subject for the fine friends, for whose good opinion Melchior had been so anxious? Do you think he was as anxious now? Do you think he was troubled by what they either saw or said? or was ashamed of the wretched prodigal lying

D

among the cushions? I think not. I think that
for the most foolish of us there are moments in
life (of real joy or real sorrow) when we judge
things by a higher standard, and care vastly
little for what 'people say.' The only shame
that Melchior felt, was that his brother should
have fared so hardly in the trials and tempta-
tions of the world outside, while he had sat at
ease among the cushions of the old coach, that
had been the home of both alike. Thank God,
it was the home of both now! And poor Hop-
o'-my-thumb was on the front seat at last, with
Melchior kneeling at his feet, and fondly stroking the head that rested against him.

"'Has powder come into fashion, Brother?'
he said. 'Your hair is streaked with white.'

"'If it has,' said the other, laughing, 'your
barber is better than mine, Melchior, for your
head is as white as snow.'

"'Is it possible? are we so old? has Time gone
so very fast? But what are you staring at through
the window? I shall be jealous of that crowd,
Brother.'

"'I am not looking at the crowd,' said the
prodigal in a low voice; 'but I see—'

"'You see what?' said Melchior.

"'A figure in a cloak, gliding in and out—'

"Melchior sprang up in horror. 'No! no!' he cried hoarsely. 'No! surely no!'

"Surely yes! Too surely the well-known figure came on; and the prodigal's sunken eyes looked more sunken still as he gazed. As for Melchior, he neither spoke nor moved, but stood in a silent agony, terrible to see. All at once a thought seemed to strike him; he seized his brother, and pushed him to the furthest corner of the seat, and then planted himself firmly at the door, just as Death came up and put his hand into the coach. Then he spoke in a low steady voice, more piteous than cries or tears.

"'I humbly beseech you, good Death, if you must take one of us, to take me. I have had a long drive, and many comforts and blessings, and am willing if unworthy to go. He has suffered much, and had no pleasure; leave him for a little to enjoy the drive in peace, just for a very little; he has suffered so much, and I have been so much to blame; let me go instead of him.'

"Alas for Melchior! It is decreed in the Providence of God, that, although the opportunities for doing good, which are in the power of every man, are beyond count or knowledge; yet, the opportunity once neglected, no man by any self-sacrifice can atone for those who have fallen or suffered by his negligence. Poor Melchior! An unalterable law made him the powerless spectator of the consequences of his neglected opportunities. 'No man may deliver his brother, or make agreement unto God for him, for it cost more to redcem their souls, so that he must let that alone for ever.' And is it ever so bitter to 'let alone,' as in a case where we might have acted and did not?

"Poor Melchior! In vain he laid both his hands in Death's outstretched palm; they fell to him again as if they had passed through air; he was pushed aside—Death passed into the coach—'one was taken and the other left.'

"As the cloaked figure glided in and out among the crowd, many turned to look at his sad burden, though few heeded him. Much was said; but the general voice of the crowd was this: 'Ah! he is gone, is he? Well! a born rascal! It must be a great relief to his brother!' A conclusion which was about as wise, and about as near the truth, as the world's conclusions generally are. As for Melchior, he neither saw the figure nor heard the crowd, for he had fallen senseless among the cushions.

"When he came to his senses, he found him-

self lying still upon his face; and so bitter was
his loneliness and grief, that he lay still and did
not move. He was astonished, however, by the
(as it seemed to him) unusual silence. The noise
of the carriages had been deafening, and now
there was not a sound. Was he deaf? or had
the crowd gone? He opened his eyes. Was he
blind? or had the night come? He sat right up,
and shook himself, and looked again. The crowd
was gone; so, for matter of that, was the coach;
and so was Godfather Time. He had not been
lying among cushions, but among pillows; he
was not in any vehicle of any kind, but in bed.
The room was dark, and very still; but through
the 'barracks' window, which had no blind, he
saw the winter sun pushing through the mist, like
a red hot cannon-ball hanging in the frosty trees;
and in the yard outside, the cocks were crowing.

"There was no longer any doubt that he was
safe in his old home; but where were his brothers and sisters? With a beating heart he
crept to the other end of the bed; and there
lay the prodigal, but with no haggard cheeks or
sunken eyes, no grey locks or miserable rags,
but a rosy yellow-haired urchin fast asleep, with
his head upon his arm. 'I took his pillow,'
muttered Melchior self-reproachfully.

"A few minutes later, young Hop-o'-my-thumb, (whom Melchior dared not lose sight of for fear he should melt away,) seated comfortably on his brother's back, and wrapped up in a blanket, was making a tour of the 'barracks.'

"'It's an awful lark,' said he, shivering with a mixture of cold and delight.

"If not exactly a *lark*, it was a very happy tour to Melchior, as, hope gradually changing into certainty, he recognized his brothers in one shapeless lump after the other in the little beds. There they all were, sleeping peacefully in a happy home, from the embryo hero, to the embryo philosopher, who lay with the invariable book upon his pillow, and his hair looking (as it always did) as if he lived in a high wind.

"'I say,' whispered Melchior, pointing to him, 'what did he say the other day about being a parson?'

"'He said he should like to be one,' returned Hop-o'-my-thumb; 'but you said he would frighten away the congregation with his looks. And then, you know, he got awful waxy, and said he didn't know priests need be dandies, and that everybody was humbuggy alike, and thought of nothing but looks; but that he would be a philosopher like Diogenes, who cared for nobody, and was as ugly as an ape, and lived in a tub.'

"'He will make a capital parson,' said Melchior hastily, 'and I shall tell him so to-morrow. And when I'm the squire here, he shall be vicar, and I'll subscribe to all his dodges without a grumble. I'm the eldest son. And I say, don't you think we could brush his hair for him in a morning, till he learns to do it himself?'

"'Oh, I will!' was the lively answer; 'I'm an awful dab at brushing. Look how I brush your best hat!'

"'True,' said Melchior. 'Where are the girls to-night?'

"'In the little room at the end of the long passage,' said Hop-o'-my-thumb, trembling with increased chilliness and enjoyment. 'But you're never going there! we shall wake the company, and they will all come out to see what's the matter.'

"'I shouldn't care if they did,' said Melchior; 'it would make it feel more real.'

"As he did not understand this sentiment, Hop-o'-my-thumb said nothing, but held on very tightly; and they crept softly down the cold grey passage in the dawn. The girls' door was open; for the girls were afraid of robbers, and left their bed-room door wide open at night, as a natural and obvious means of self-defence. The girls slept together; and the frill of the pale sister's prim little night-cap was buried in the other one's uncovered curls.

" 'How you do tremble!' whispered Hop-o'-my-thumb; 'are you cold?' This inquiry received no answer; and after some minutes he spoke again. 'I say, how awfully pretty they look! don't they?'

"But for some reason or other, Melchior seemed to have lost his voice; but he stooped down and kissed both the girls very gently, and then the two brothers crept back along the passage to the 'barracks.'

" 'One thing more,' said Melchior; and they went up to the mantelpiece. 'I will lend you my bow and arrows to-morrow, on one condition—'

" 'Anything!' was the reply, in an enthusiastic whisper.

" 'That you take that old picture for a target, and never let me see it again.'

"It was very ungrateful! but perfection is not in man; and there was something in Melchior's muttered excuse—

" 'I couldn't stand another night of it.'

" Hop-o'-my-thumb was speedily put to bed again, to get warm, this time with both the pillows ; but Melchior was too restless to sleep, so he resolved to have a shower-bath and to dress. After which he knelt down by the window, and covered his face with his hands.

" ' He's saying very long prayers,' thought Hop-o'-my-thumb, squinting at him from his warm nest; 'and what a jolly humour he is in this morning !'

" Still the young head was bent, and the handsome face hidden ; and Melchior was finding his life every moment more real and more happy. For there was hardly a thing, from the well-filled ' barracks ' to the brother bedfellow, that had been a hardship last night, which this morning did not seem a blessing. He rose at last, and stood in the sunshine, which was now pouring in ; a smile was on his lips, and on his face were two drops, which, if they were water, had not come from the shower-bath, or from any bath at all."

. . . .

" Is that the end ?" inquired the young lady on his knee, as the story-teller paused here.

" Yes, that is the end."

" It's a beautiful story," she murmured

thoughtfully; " but what an extraordinary one ! I don't think I could have dreamt such a wonderful dream."

" Do you think you could have eaten such a wonderful supper?" said the friend, twisting his moustachios.

After this, the whole evening was what the French would term " a grand success." Richard took his smoking boots from the fire-place, and was called upon for various entertainments for which he was famous; such as the accurate imitation of a train just starting, in which two pieces of bone were used with considerable effect; as also of a bumble-bee, who (very much out of season) went buzzing about, and was always being caught with a heavy bang on the heads and shoulders of those who least expected it; all which specimens of his talents were received with due applause by his admiring brothers and sisters.

The bumble-bee had just been caught (for the twenty-first time) with a loud smack on brother Benjamin's ear, when the door opened, and Paterfamilias entered with Materfamilias (whose headache was better), and followed by the candles. A fresh log was then thrown upon the fire, the yule cakes and furmety were put

upon the table, and everybody drew round to
supper; and Paterfamilias announced that although he could not give the materials to play
with, he had no objection now to a bowl of
moderate punch for all, and that Richard might
compound it. This was delightful; and as he sat
by his father ladling away to the rest, Adolphus
Brown could hardly have felt more jovial, even
with the champagne and ices.

The rest sat with radiant faces and shining
heads in goodly order; and at the bottom of
the table, by Materfamilias, was the friend, as
happy in his unselfish sympathy as if his twenty-
five sticks had come to life, and were supping
with him. As happy—nearly—as if a certain
woman's grave had never been dug under the
southern sun that could not save her, and as if
the children gathered round him were those, of
whose faces he had often dreamt, but might
never see.

His health had been drunk, and everybody
else's too, when just as supper was coming to a
close, Richard (who had been sitting in thought-
ful silence for some minutes) got up with sudden
resolution, and said,

" I want to propose Mr. What's-his-name's
health on my own account. I want to thank

him for his story, which had only one mistake
in it. Melchior should have kept the effervescing papers to put into the beer; it's a splendid
drink! Otherwise it was first-rate; though it
hit me rather hard. I want to say that though
I didn't mean all I said about being an only
son, (when a fellow gets put out he doesn't
know what he means,) yet I know I was quite
wrong, and the story is quite right. I want particularly to say that I'm very glad there are so
many of us, for the more, you know, the mer-
rier. I wouldn't change father or mother, brothers or sisters, with any one in the world. It
couldn't be better, we couldn't be happier. We
are all together, and to-morrow is Christmas
Day. Thank GOD."

It was very well said. It was a very good
speech. It was very well and very good, that
while the blessings were with him, he could feel
it to be so, and be grateful.

It was very well, and good also, that the
friend, who had neither home nor kindred to
be grateful for, had something else for which he
could thank GOD as heartily. The thought of
that something came to him then as he sat at his
friend's table, filling his eyes with tears. It came
to him next day as he knelt before GOD's altar,

remembering in blessed fellowship that deed of love, which is the foundation of all our hope and joy. It came to him when he went back to his lonely wandering life, and thought with tender interest of that boyish speech. It came—a whisper of consolation to silence envy and regret for ever.

"There *is* something far better. There *is* something far happier. There is a better Home than any earthly one, and a Family that shall never be divided."

THE BLACKBIRD'S NEST.

"Let me not think an action mine own way,
But as Thy love shall sway,
Resigning up the rudder to Thy skill."

GEORGE HERBERT.

ONE day, when I was a very little girl (which is a long time ago), I made a discovery. The place where I made it was not very remote, being a holly-bush at the bottom of our garden; and the discovery was not a great one in itself, though I thought it very grand. I had found a blackbird's nest, with three young ones in it.

The discovery was made on this wise. I was sitting one morning on a log of wood opposite this holly-bush, reading the story of Goody Twoshoes, and thinking to myself how much I should like to be like her, and to go about in the village with a raven, a pigeon, and a lark, on my shoulders, admired and talked about by everybody. All sorts of nonsense passed through my head as I sat, with the book on my lap, staring straight before me; and I was just

THE BLACKBIRD'S GRAVE.

fancying the kind condescension with which I would behave to everybody, when I became a Goody Twoshoes, when I saw a bird come out of the holly-bush and fly away. It was a blackbird; there was no doubt of it: and it must have a nest in the tree, or why had it been there so long? Down went my book, and I flew to make my discovery. A blackbird's nest, with three young ones! I stood still at first in pure pleasure at the sight; and then, little by little, grand ideas came into my head.

I would be very kind to these little blackbirds (I thought); I would take them home out of this cold tree, and make a large nest of cotton wool, (which would be much softer and better for them than to be where they were,) and feed them, and keep them; and then when they were full grown, they would, of course, love me better than any one, and be very tame and grateful; and I should walk about with them on my shoulders like Goody Twoshoes, and be admired by everybody; for I am ashamed to say, most of my day dreams ended with this, *to be admired by everybody.* I was so wrapped up in these thoughts, that I did not know, till his hands were laid upon my shoulders, that my friend, the curate of the village, had come up behind me. He lived next door to us, and often climbed over the wall that divided our garden, to bring me flowers for my little bed. He was a tall, dark, not very young man; and the best hand at making fire-balloons, mending toys, and making a broken wax doll as good as new with a hot knitting-needle, that you can imagine. I had heard grown-up people call him grave and silent, but he always laughed and talked to me.

"What are you doing, little woman?" he said.

"I have got a nest of poor little birds," I answered; "I am so sorry for them here in the cold; but they will be all right when I have got them indoors. I shall make them a beautiful nest of cotton wool, and feed them. Won't it be nice?"

I spoke confidently; for I had really so worked up my fancy, that I felt quite a contemptuous pity for all the wretched little birds who were hatched every year without me to rear them. At the same time I had a general idea that grown-up people always *did* throw cold water on splendid plans like mine; so I was more indignant than surprised when my friend the curate tried to show me that it was quite impossible to do as I wished. The end of all his arguments was, that I must leave the nest in its place. But I had a great turn for disputing, and was not at all inclined to give up my point. "You told me on Sunday," I said pertly, "that we were never too little to do kind things; let me do this."

"If I could be sure," he said, looking at me, "that you only wish to do a kind thing."

I got more angry and rude.

"Perhaps you think I want to kill them," I said.

He did not answer, but taking both my hands in his, said gravely, "Tell me, my child, which do you wish most—to be kind to these poor little birds? or to have the honour and glory of having them, and bringing them up?"

"To be kind to them," said I, getting very red. "I don't want any honour and glory," and I felt ready to cry.

"Well, well," he said, smiling; "then I know you will believe me when I tell you, that the kindest thing you can do for these little birds is to leave them where they are. And if you like, you can come and sit here every day till they are able to fly, and keep watch over the nest, that no naughty boy may come near it—

E

the curate, for instance!" and he pulled a funny face. "That will be very kind."

"But they will never know, and I want them to like me," said I.

"I thought you only wanted to be kind," he answered. And then he began to talk very gently about different sorts of kindness, and that if I wished to be kind like a Christian, I must be kind without hoping for any reward, whether gratitude or anything else. He told me that the best followers of Jesus in all times had tried hard to do everything, however small, simply for GOD's sake, and to put themselves away. That they often began even their letters, etc., with such words, as, " Glory to GOD," to remind themselves that everything they did, to be perfect, must be done to GOD, and GOD alone. And that in doing good kind things even, they were afraid lest, though the thing was right, the wish to do it might have come from conceit or presumption.

"This self-devotion," he added, "is the very highest Christian life, and seems, I dare say, very hard for you even to understand, and much more so to put in practice. But we must all try for it in the best way we can, little woman; and to those who by GOD's grace really practised it, it was almost as impossible to be downcast or disappointed as if they were already in Heaven. They wished for nothing to happen to themselves but God's will; they did nothing but for God's glory. And so a very good bishop says, ' I have my end, whether I succeed or am disappointed.' So you will have your end, my child, in being kind to these little birds in the right way, and denying yourself, whether they know you or not."

I could not have understood all he said; but I am afraid I did not try to understand what I might have done; however, I said no more, and stood silent, while he comforted me with the promise of a new flower for my garden, called " hen and chickens," which he said I was to take care of instead of the little blackbirds.

When he was gone I went back to the holly-bush, and stood gazing at the nest, and nursing angry thoughts in my heart. " What a *preach*," I thought, " about nothing! as if there could be any conceit and presumption in taking care of three poor little birds! The curate must forget that I was growing into a big girl; and as to not knowing how to feed them, I knew as well as he did that birds lived upon worms, and liked bread-crumbs." And so *thinking wrong* ended (as it almost always does) in *doing wrong :* and I took the three little blackbirds out of the nest, popped them into my pocket-handkerchief, and ran home. And some trouble I took to keep them out of every one's sight—even out of my mother's; for I did not want to hear any more "grown-up" opinions on the matter.

I filled a basket with cotton wool, and put the birds inside, and took them into a little room down-stairs, where they would be warm. Before I went to bed I put two or three worms, and a large supply of soaked bread-crumbs, in the nest, close to their little beaks. "What can they want more?" thought I in my folly; but conscience is apt to be restless when one is young, and I could not feel quite comfortable in bed, though I got to sleep at last, trying to fancy myself Goody Twoshoes, with three sleek full-fledged blackbirds on my shoulders.

In the morning, as soon as I could slip away, I went to my pets. Any one may guess what I found; but I believe no one can understand the shock of agony and remorse that I felt. There lay the worms that I had dug up with reckless cruelty; there was the wasted bread; and there, above all, lay the three little blackbirds, cold and dead !

I do not know how long I stood looking at the victims of my presumptuous wilfulness; but at last I heard a footstep in the passage, and fearing to be caught, I tore out of the house, and down to my old seat near the holly-bush, where I flung myself on the ground, and " wept bitterly." At last I heard the well-known sound of some one climbing over the wall; and then the curate stood before me, with the plant of " hen and chickens " in his hands. I jumped up, and shrank away from him.

"Don't come near me," I cried; " the blackbirds are dead;" and I threw myself down again.

I knew from experience that few things roused the anger of my friend so strongly as to see or hear of animals being ill-treated. I had never forgotten, one day when I was out with him, his wrath over a boy who was cruelly beating a donkey; and now I felt, though I could not see, the expression of his face, as he looked at the holly-bush and at me, and exclaimed, " You took them!" And then added, in the low tone in which he always spoke when angry, " And the mother-bird has been wandering all night round this tree, seeking her little ones in vain, not to be comforted, because they are not!

Child, child ! has God the Father given life to
His creatures for you to destroy it in this reckless manner?"

His words cut my heart like a knife; but I
was too utterly wretched already to be much
more miserable; I only lay still and moaned.
At last he took pity, and lifting me up on to
his knee, endeavoured to comfort me.

This was not, however, any easy matter. I
knew much better than he did how very naughty
I had been; and I felt that I had murdered the
poor tender little birds.

"I can never, never, forgive myself!" I
sobbed.

"But you must be reasonable," he said.
"You gave way to your vanity and wilfulness,
and persuaded yourself that you only wished to
be kind to the blackbirds; and you have been
punished.   Is it not so?"

"O yes!" I cried; "I am so wicked!   I
wish I were as good as you are!"

"As I am!"—he began.

I was too young then to understand the sharp
tone of self-reproach in which he spoke. In my
eyes he was perfection; only perhaps a little
too good.   But he went on:—

"Do you know, this fault of yours reminds

me of a time when I was just as wilful and conceited, just as much bent upon doing the great duty of helping others in my own grand fashion, rather than in the humble way in which God's Providence pointed out, only it was in a much more serious matter; I was older too, and so had less excuse. I am almost tempted to tell you about it; not that our cases are really quite alike, but that the punishment which met my sin was so unspeakably bitter in comparison with yours, that you may be thankful to have learnt a lesson of humility at smaller cost."

I did not understand him—in fact, I did not understand many things that he said, for he had a habit of talking to me as if he were speaking to himself; but I had a general idea of his meaning, and said, (very truly,) "I cannot fancy you doing wrong."

I was puzzled again by the curious expression of his face; but he only said, "Shall I tell you a story?"

I knew his stories of old, and gave an eager "Yes."

"It is a sad one," he said.

"I do not think I should like a very funny one just now," I replied. "Is it true?"

"Quite," he answered. "It is about my-self." He was silent for a few moments, as if making up his mind to speak; and then, laying his head, as he sometimes did, on my shoulder, so that I could not see his face, he began.

"When I was a boy, (older than you, so I ought to have been better,) I might have been described in the words of Scripture. I was 'the only son of my mother, and she was a widow.' We were badly off, and she was very delicate, nay, ill—more ill, GOD knows, than I had any idea of. I had long been used to the sight of the doctor once or twice a week, and to her being sometimes better and some-times worse; and when our old servant lectured me for making a noise, or the doctor begged that she might not be excited or worried, I fancied that doctors and nurses always did say things of that sort, and that there was no parti-cular need to attend to them.

"Not that I was unfeeling to my dear mother, for I loved her devotedly in my wilful worldly way. It was for her sake that I had been so vexed by the poverty into which my father's death had plunged us. For her sake I worried her, by grumbling before her at our narrow lodgings and lost comforts. For her sake, child, in my madness, I wasted the hours in which I might have soothed, and comforted, and waited on her, in dreaming of wild schemes for making myself famous and rich, and giving her back all and more than she had lost. For her sake I fancied myself pouring money at her feet, and loading her with luxuries, while she was praying for me to our common Father, and laying up treasure for herself in Heaven.

"One day I remember, when she was remonstrating with me over a bad report which the schoolmaster had given of me, (he said I could work, but wouldn't,) my vanity overcame my prudence, and I told her that I thought some fellows were made to 'fag,' and some not; that I had been writing a poem in my dictionary the day that I had done so badly, and that I hoped to be a poet long before my master had composed a grammar. I can see now her sorrowful face as, with tears in her eyes, she told me that all 'fellows' alike were made to do their duty 'before GOD, and Angels, and Men.' That it was by improving the little events and opportunities of every day that men became great, and not by neglecting them for their own presumptuous fancies. And she entreated me to strive to do my duty, and to leave the rest with God. I listened, however, impatiently to what I called a 'jaw' or a 'scold,' and then (knowing the tender interest she took in all I did) I tried to coax her by offering to read my poem. But she answered with just severity, that what she wished was to see me a good man, not a great one; and that she would rather see my exercises duly written than fifty poems composed at the expense of my neglected duty. Then she warned me tenderly of the misery which my conceit would bring upon me, and bade me, when I said my evening prayers, to add that prayer of King David, 'Keep Thy servant from presumptuous sins, lest they get the dominion over me.'

"Alas! they had got the dominion over me already, too strongly for her words to take any hold. 'She won't even look at my poem,' I thought, and hurried proudly from the room, banging one door and leaving another open. And I silenced my uneasy conscience by fresh dreams of making my fortune and hers. But the punishment came at last. One day the doctor took me into a room alone, and told me as gently as he could what every one but myself knew already—my mother was dying. I cannot tell you, child, how the blow fell upon me—

how, at first, I utterly disbelieved its truth! It seemed *impossible* that the only hope of my life, the object of all my schemes and fancies, was to be taken away. But I was awakened at last, and resolved that, GOD helping me, while she did live, I would be a better son. I can now look back with thankfulness on the few days we were together. I never left her. She took her food and medicine from my hand; and I received my First Communion with her on the day she died. The day before, kneeling by her bed, I had confessed all the sin and vanity of my heart and those miserable dreams; had destroyed with my own hand all my papers, and had resolved that I would apply to my studies, and endeavour to obtain a scholarship and the necessary preparation for Holy Orders. It was a just ambition, little woman, undertaken humbly, in the fear of GOD, and in the path of duty; and I accomplished it years after, when I had nothing left of my mother but her memory."

The curate was silent, and I felt, rather than saw, that the tears which were wetting my frock had not come from my own eyes, though I was crying bitterly. I flung my arms round his neck, and hugged him tight.

"Oh, I am so sorry!" I sobbed; "so very, very sorry!"

We became quieter after a bit; and he lifted up his head and smiled, and called himself a fool for making me sad, and told me not to tell any one what he had told me, and what babies we had been, except my mother.

"Tell her *everything* always," he said.

I soon cheered up, particularly as he took me over the wall, and into his workshop, and made a coffin for the poor little blackbirds, which we lined with cotton-wool and scented with musk, as a mark of respect. Then he dug a deep hole in the garden and we buried them, and made a fine high mound of earth, and put the "hen and chicken" plants all round. And that night, sitting on my mother's knee, I told her "everything," and shed a few more tears of sorrow and repentance in her arms.

.   .   .   .

Many years have passed since then, and many showers of rain have helped to lay the mound flat with the earth, so that "hen and chickens" has run all over it, and made a fine plot. The curate and his mother have met at last; and I have transplanted many flowers that he gave me to his grave. I sometimes wonder if, in his perfect happiness, he knows, or cares to know, how often the remembrance of his story has stopped the current of conceited day-dreams, and brought me back to practical duty with the humble prayer, " Keep Thy servant also from presumptuous sins."

62

FRIEDRICH'S BALLAD.

A TALE OF THE FEAST OF ST. NICHOLAS.

"Nè pinger nè scolpir fia più che queti,
L'anima volta a quell' Amor divino
Ch'asserse a prender noi in Croce le braccia."

Painting and Sculpture's aid in vain I crave,
My one sole refuge is that Love divine
Which from the Cross stretched forth its arms to save."

Written by MICHAEL ANGELO *at the age of* 83.

"So be it," said one of the council, as he rose
and addressed the others. "It is now finally
decided. The Story Woman is to be walled
up."

The council was not an ecclesiastical one, and
the woman condemned to the barbarous and by-
gone punishment of being "walled up" was not
an offending nun. In fact the Story Woman (or
Märchen-Frau as she is called in Germany)
may be taken to represent the imaginary per-
sonage who is known in England by the name
of Mother Bunch, or Mother Goose; and
it was in this instance the name given by a

THE EVE OF ST NICHOLAS.

certain family of children to an old book of
ballads and poems, which they were accustomed
to read in turn with special solemnities, on one
particular night in the year; the reader for the
time being having a peculiar costume, and the
title of 'Märchen-Frau,' or Mother Bunch, a
name which had in time been familiarly adopted
for the ballad-book itself.

This book was not bound in a fashionable
colour, nor illustrated by a fashionable artist;
the Chiswick Press had not set up a type for it,
and Hayday's morocco was a thing unknown.
It had not, in short, one of those attractions
with which in these days books are surrounded,
whose insides do not always fulfil the promise of
the binding. If, however, it was on these points
inferior to modern volumes, it had on others the
advantage. It did not share a precarious favour
with a dozen other rivals in mauve, to be sup-
planted ere the year was out by twelve new
ones in magenta. It was never thrown aside with
the contemptuous remark,—" I've read that!"
On the contrary, it always had been to its pos-
sessors what (from the best Book downwards) a
good book always should be, a friend, and not
an acquaintance,—not to be too readily criti-
cized, but to be loved and trusted. The pages

were yellow and worn, not with profane ill-usage, but with honourable wear and tear; and the mottled binding presented much such an appearance as might be expected from a book that had been pressed under the pillow of one reader, and in the pocket of another; that had been wept over and laughed over, and warmed by winter fires, and damped in the summer grass, and had in general seen as much of life as the venerable book in question. It was not the property of one member of the family, but the joint possession of all. It was not *mine*, but *ours*, as the inscription, " For the Children," written on the blank leaf testified; which inscription was hereafter to be a pathetic memorial to aged eyes of days when "the children" were not yet separated, and took their pleasures, like their meals, together.

And after all this, with the full consent of a council of the owners, the *Märchen-Frau* was to be " walled up."

But before I attempt to explain, or in any way excuse this seemingly ungracious act, it may be well to give some account of the doers thereof. Well, then :—

Providence had blessed a certain respectable tradesman, in a certain town in Germany, with a large and promising family of children. He had married very early the beloved of his boyhood, and had been left a widower with one motherless baby almost before he was a man. A neighbour, with womanly compassion, took pity upon this desolate father, and more desolate child; and it was not until she had nursed the babe in her own house through a dangerous sickness, and had for long been chief adviser to the parent, that he awoke to the fact that she had become necessary to him, and they were married.

Of this union came a family of eight, the two eldest of whom were laid in turn in the quiet grave. The others survived, and, with the first wife's daughter, made a goodly family party, which sometimes sorely taxed the resources of the tradesman to provide for, though his business was good and his wife careful. They scrambled up, however, as children are wont to do under such circumstances; and at the time our story opens the youngest had turned his back upon babyhood, and Marie, the eldest, had reached that pinnacle of childish ambition,—she was " grown up."

A very good Marie she was, and always had been; from the days when she ran to school with a little knapsack on her back, and her fair hair

F

hanging down in two long plaits, to the present time, when she tenderly fastened that same knapsack on to the shoulders of a younger sister; and when the plaits had for long been reclaimed from their vagrant freedom, and coiled close to her head.

"Our Marie is not clever," said one of the children, who flattered himself that *he was* a bit of a genius; "our Marie is not clever, but also she is never wrong."

It is with this same genius that our story has chiefly to do.

Friedrich was a child of unusual talent; a fact which, happily for himself, was not discovered till he was more than twelve years old. He learnt to read very quickly; and when he was once able, read every book on which he could lay his hands, and in his father's house the number was not great. When Marie was a child, the school was kept by a certain old man, very gentle and learned in his quiet way. He had been fond of his fair-haired pupil, and when she was no longer a scholar, had passed many an odd hour in imparting to her a slight knowledge of Latin, and of the great Linnæus's system of botany. He was now dead, and his place filled by a less sympathizing pedagogue; and

Friedrich listened with envious ears to his more fortunate sister's stories of her friend and master.

"So he taught you Latin,—that great language! And botany,—which is a science!" the child would exclaim with envious admiration, when he had heard for the thousandth time every particular of the old schoolmaster's kindness.

And Marie would answer calmly, as she "refooted" one of the father's stockings, "We did a good deal of the grammar, which I fear I have forgotten, and I learnt by heart a few of the Psalms in Latin, which I remember well. Also we commenced the system of Mr. Linnæus, but I was very stupid, and ever preferred those plates which pictured the flower itself to those which gave the torn pieces, and which he thought most valuable. But, above all, he taught me to be good; and though I have forgotten many of his lessons, there are words and advice of his which I heeded little then, but which come back and teach me now. Father once heard the Burgomaster say he was a genius, but I know that he was good, and that is best of all;" with which, having turned the heel of her stocking, Marie would put it out of reach of the kitten, and lay the table for dinner.

And Friedrich—poor Friedrich!—groaning

inwardly at his sister's indifference to her great
opportunities for learning, would speculate to
himself on the probable fate of each volume in
the old schoolmaster's library, which had been
sold when he, Friedrich, was but three years
old.   Under these circumstances, the boy expressed his feelings with moderation when he
said, " Our Marie is not clever, but also she is
never wrong."

If the schoolmaster was dead, however, Friedrich was not, nevertheless, friendless.   There
was a certain bookseller in his native town, for
whom in his spare time he ran messages, and
who in return was glad to let him spend his
playhours and half-holidays among the books
in his shop.   There, perched at the top of the
shelves on a ladder, or crouched upon his toes
at the bottom, he devoured some volumes and
dipped into others ; but what he liked best was
poetry, and this not uncommon taste with
many young readers was with this one a mania.
Wherever the sight of verses met his eye, there
he fastened and read greedily.

One day, a short time before my story opens,
he found, in his wanderings from shelf to shelf,
some nicely-bound volumes, one of which he
opened, and straightway verses of the most at-

tractive-looking metre met his eye, but not in German, but a fair round Roman text, and, alas! in a language which he did not understand. There were customers in the shop, so he stood still in the corner with his nose almost resting on the bookshelf, and staring fiercely at the page, as if he would force the meaning out of those fair clear-looking verses. When the last beard had vanished through the doorway, Friedrich came up to the counter, book in hand.

"Well, now?" said the comfortable bookseller, with a round German smile.

"This book," said the boy; "in what language is it?"

The man stuck his spectacles on his nose, and smiled again.

"It is Italian, and these are the sonnets of Petrarch, my child. The edition is a fine one, so be careful." Friedrich went back to his place, sighing heavily. After a while he came out again.

"Well now, what is it?" said the bookseller, cheerfully.

"Have you an Italian grammar?"

"Only this," said the other, as he picked a book from the shelf and laid it on the counter with a twinkle in his eye. The boy opened it and looked up disappointed.

" It is all Italian," said he.

" No, no," was the answer; " it is in French
and Italian, and was printed at Paris. But
what wouldst thou with a grammar, my child?"

The boy blushed as if he had been caught
stealing, and said hastily,—

" I *must* read those poems, and I cannot if I
do not learn the language."

"And thou wouldst read Petrarch with a
grammar," shouted the bookseller; " ho! ho!
ho!"

"And a dictionary," said Friedrich; "why
not?"

" Why not?" repeated the other, with renewed
laughter. " Why not? Because to learn a language, my Friedrich, one must have a master,
and exercises, and a phrase-book, and progressive reading-lessons with vocabulary; and in
short, one must learn a language in the way
everybody else learns it; that is why not, my
Friedrich."

" Everybody is nobody," said Friedrich hotly;
" at least nobody worth caring for. If I had a
grammar and a dictionary, I would read those
beautiful poems."

" Hear him!" said the cheerful little bookseller. " He will read Petrarch. He! If my

volumes stop in the shelves till thou canst read them, my child—ho! ho! ho!" and he rubbed his brushy little beard with glee.

Friedrich's temper was not by nature of the calmest, and this conversation rubbed its tenderest points. He answered almost fiercely,—

"Take care of your volumes. If I live, and they *do* stop in the shelves, I will buy them of you some day. Remember!" and he turned sharply round to hide the tears which had begun to fall.

For a moment the good shopkeeper's little mouth became as round as his round little eyes and his round little face; then he laid his hands on the counter, and jumping neatly over flung his dead weight on to Friedrich, and embraced him heartily.

"My poor child! (a kiss)—would that it had pleased Heaven to make thee the son of a nobleman—(another kiss). But hear me. A man in Berlin is now compiling an Italian grammar. It is to be out in a month or two. I shall have a copy, and thou shalt see it; and if ever thou canst read Petrarch I will give thee my volumes —(a volley of kisses.) And now, as thou hast stayed so long, come into the little room and dine with me." With which invitation the kind-

hearted German released his young friend and
led him into the back room, where they buried
the memory of Petrarch in a mess of vegetables
and melted butter.   .

It may be added here, that the Petrarchs remained on the shelf, and that years afterwards
the round-faced little bookseller redeemed his
promise with pride.

Of these visits the father was to all intents
and purposes ignorant. He knew that Friedrich
went to see the bookseller, and that the bookseller was goodnatured to him ; but he never
dreamt that his son read the books with which
his neighbour's shop was lined, and he knew nothing of the wild visions which that same shop
bred and nourished in the mind of his boy, and
which made the life outside its doorstep seem a
dream.   The father and son saw that life from
different points of view.   The boy felt that he
was more talented than other boys, and designed
himself for a poet ; the tradesman saw that the
boy was more talented than other boys, and designed him for the business ; and the opposite
nature of these determinations was the one great
misery of Friedrich's life.

If, however, this source of the child's sorrows
was a secret one, and not spoken of to his bro-

thers and sisters, or even to his friend the bookseller, equally secret also were the sources of his
happiness. No eye but his own ever beheld
those scraps of paper which he begged from the
bookseller, and covered with childish efforts at
verse-making. No one shared the happiness of
those hours, of which perhaps a quarter was
spent in working at the poem, and three-fourths
were given to the day-dreams of the poet; or
knew that the wild fancies of his brain made
Friedrich's nights more happy than his days.
By day he was a child, (his family, with some
reason, said a tiresome one,) by night he was a
man, and a great man. He visited the courts
of Europe, and received compliments from Royalty; *his* plays were acted in the theatres; *his*
poems stood on the shelves of the booksellers;
he made his family rich, (the boy was too
young to wish for money for himself); he made
everybody happy, and himself famous.

Fame! that was the word that rang in his
ears and danced before his eyes as the hours of
the night wore on, and he lived through a glorious lifetime. And so when the mother, candle
in hand, came round like a guardian angel among
the sleeping children, to see that " all was right,"
he—poor child !—must feign to be sleeping on

his face, to hide the traces of the tears which he
had wept as he composed the epitaph which was
to grace the monument of the famous Friedrich
——, poet, philosopher, etc.   Whoever doubts
the possibility of such exaggerated folly, has
never known an imaginative childhood, or wept
over those unreal griefs, which are not the less
bitter at the time from being remembered afterwards with a mixture of shame and amusement.
Happy or unhappy, however, in his dreams, the
boy was great, and this was enough; for Friedrich was vain, as every one is tempted to be who
feels himself in any way singular and unlike
those about him.   He revelled in the honours
which he showered upon himself, and so—the
night was happy ; and so—the day was unwel-
come when he was smartly bid to get up and
put on his stockings, and found Fame gone and
himself a child again, without honour, in his
own country, and in his father's house.

These sad dreams (sad in their uselessness)
were destined however to do him some good
at last ; and, oddly enough, the childish council
that condemned the ballad-book decided his fate
also.   This was how it happened.

The children were accustomed, as we have
said, to celebrate the Feast of St. Nicholas by

readings from their beloved book. St. Nicholas's Day (the 6th of December) has for years been a favourite festival with the children in many parts of the Continent. In France, the children are diligently taught that St. Nicholas comes in the night down the chimney, and fills the little shoes (which are ranged there for the purpose) with sweetmeats or rods, according to his opinion of their owner's conduct during the past year. The Saint is supposed to travel through the air, and to be followed by an ass laden with two panniers, one of which contains the good things, and the other the birch, and he leaves his ass at the top of the chimney and comes down alone. The same belief is entertained in Holland; and in some parts of Germany he is even believed to carry off bad boys and girls in his sack, answering in this respect to our English Bogy.

The day, as may be supposed, is looked forward to with no small amount of anxiety; very clean and tidy are the little shoes placed by the young expectants; and their parents—who have threatened and promised in St. Nicholas's name for a year past—take care that, with one sort of present or the other, the shoes are well filled. The great question—rods or sweetmeats

—is, however, finally settled for each individual before breakfast-time on the great day; and before dinner, despite maternal warnings, most of the said sweetmeats have been consumed. And so it came to pass that Friedrich and his brothers and sisters had hit upon a plan for ending the day, with the same spirit and enjoyment with which it opened.

The mother, by a little kind manœuvring, generally induced the father to sup and take his evening pipe with a neighbour, for the tradesman was one of those whose presence is rather a "wet blanket" upon all innocent folly and fun. Then she goodnaturedly took herself off to household matters, and the children were left in undisturbed possession of the stove, round which they gathered with the book, and the game commenced. Each in turn read whichever poem he preferred; and the reader for the time being, was wrapt in a huge hood and cloak, kept for the purpose, and was called the ' Märchen-Frau,' or Story Woman. Sometimes the song had a chorus, which all the children sang to whichever suited best of the thousand airs that are always floating in German brains. Sometimes, if the ballad was a favourite one, the others would take part in any verses that contained a dialogue. This was generally the case with some verses in the pet ballad of Bluebeard, at that exciting point where sister Anne is looking from the castle window. First the Märchen-Frau read in a sonorous voice—

" Schwester Aennchen, siehst du nichts ?"
(Sister Anne, do you see nothing?)

Then the others replied for Anne—

" Stäubchen fliegen, Gräschen wehen."
(A little dust flies, a little grass waves.)

Again the Märchen-Frau—

" Aennchen, lässt sich sonst nichts sehen?"
(Little Anne, is there nothing else to be seen?)

And the unsatisfactory reply—

"Schwesterchen, sonst seh' ich nichts!"
(Little sister, I see nothing else!)

After this the Märchen-Frau finished the ballad alone, and the conclusion was received with shouts of applause and laughter, that would have considerably astonished the good father, could he have heard them, and that did sometimes oblige the mother to call order from the loft above, just for propriety's sake; for, in truth, the good woman loved to hear them, and often hummed in with a chorus to herself as she

turned over the clothes among which she was
busy.

At last, however, after having been for
years the crowning enjoyment of St. Nicholas's
Day, the credit of the Märchen-Frau was doomed
to fade. The last reading had been rather a
failure, not because the old ballad-book was sup-
planted by a new one, or because the children
had outgrown its histories; perhaps—though
they did not acknowledge it—Friedrich was in
some degree to blame.

His increasing knowledge, the long readings
in the bookseller's shop, which his brothers and
sisters neither shared nor knew of, had given
him a feeling of contempt for the one book on
which they feasted from year to year; and his
part, as Märchen-Frau, had been on this occasion more remarkable for yawns than for anything else. The effect of this failure was not
confined to that day. Whenever the book was
brought out, there was the same feeling that the
magic of it was gone, and very greatly were the
poor children disquieted by the fact.

At last, one summer's day, in the year of
which we are writing, one of the boys was
struck, as he fancied, by a brilliant idea; and
as brilliant ideas on any subject are precious, he

lost no time in summoning a council of his brothers and sisters in the garden. It was a half-holiday, and they soon came trooping round the great linden tree—where the bees were already in full possession—and the youngest girl, who was but six years old, bore the book hugged fast in her two arms.

The boy opened the case—as lawyers say— by describing the loss of interest in their book since the last Feast of St. Nicholas. "This did not," he said, "arise from any want of love to the stories themselves, but from the fact of their knowing them so well. Whatever ballad the Märchen-Frau chose, every line of it was so familiar to each one of them that it seemed folly to repeat it. Under these circumstances it was evident that the greatest compliment they could pay the stories was to forget them, and he had a plan for attaining this desirable end. Let them deny themselves now for their future pleasure ; let them put away the Märchen-Frau till next St. Nicholas's Day, and in the meantime let each of them do his best to forget as much of it as he possibly could." The speaker ceased, and in the silence the bees above droned as if in answer, and then the children below shouted applause until the garden rang.

But now came the question, where was the
Märchen-Frau to be put? and for this the suggestive brother had also an idea. He had found
certain bricks in the thick old garden wall
which were loose, and when taken out there was
a hole which was quite the thing for their purpose. Let them wrap the book carefully up,
put it in the hole, and replace the bricks. This
was his proposal, and he sat down. The bees
droned above, the children shouted below, and
the proposal was carried amid general satisfaction. "So be it," said the suggestor, in
conclusion. "It is now finally decided. The
Märchen-Frau is to be walled up."

And walled up she was forthwith, but not
without a parting embrace from each of her
judges, and possibly some slight latent faith in
the suggestion of one of the party that perhaps
St. Nicholas would put a new inside and new
stories into her before next December.

"I don't think I should like a new inside,
though," doubted the child before mentioned,
with a shake of her tiny plaits, "or new stories
either."

As this quaint little Fräulein went into the
house she met Friedrich, who came from the
bookseller's.

" Friedrich," said she, in a solemn voice, " we have walled up the ' Märchen-Frau.' "

" Have you, *Schwesterchen ?*"

This was Friedrich's answer; but it may safely be stated that, if any one had asked him what it was that his sister had told him, he would have been utterly unable to reply.

He had been to the bookseller's !

The summer passed, and the children kept faithfully to their resolve. The little sister sometimes sat by the wall and comforted the Märchen-Frau inside, with promises of coming out soon; but not a brick was touched. There was something pathetic in the children's voluntary renouncement of their one toy. The father was too absent, and the mother too busy, to notice its loss; Marie missed it and made inquiries of the children, but she was implored to be silent, and discreetly held her tongue. Winter drew on, and for some time a change was visible in the manners of one of the children; he seemed restless and uncomfortable, as if something preyed upon his mind. At last he was induced to unburden himself to the others, when it was discovered that he couldn't forget the poems in ' Märchen-Frau.' This was the grievance.

" It seems as if I did it on purpose,"

G

groaned he in self-indignation. "The nearer
the time comes, and the more I try to forget,
the clearer I remember them every one. You
know my pet is Bluebeard; well, I thought I
would forget that altogether, every word; and
then when my turn came to be Märchen-Frau
I would take it for my piece. And now, of all
the rest, this is just the one that runs in my
head. It is quite as if I did it on purpose."

Involuntarily the company—who appeared to
have forgotten it as little as he—struck up in a
merry tune—

"Blaubart war ein reicher Mann," etc.*

"Oh, don't!" groaned the victim. "That's
just how it goes in my head all along, especially
the verse—

> "Stark war seines Körpers Bau,
>   Feurig waren seine Blicke,
>   Aber ach!—ein Missgeschicke!—
>   Aber ach! sein Bart war blau."†

"On Sunday, when the preacher gave out the
text, I was looking at him, and it came so

---

* "Bluebeard was a rich man."
† "Strong was the build of his body,
    Fiery were his glances,
    But ah!—disaster!—
    But ah! his beard was blue."

strongly into my head that I nearly said it out loud—' But, ah! his beard was blue!' To-day the schoolmaster asked me a question about Solomon. I could remember nothing but ' Ah! his beard was blue!' I have tried this week with all my might; and the harder I try, the better I remember every word. It is dreadful."

It was dreadful; but he was somewhat comforted to learn that the memories of his brothers and sisters were as perverse as his own. Those ballads were not to be easily forgotten. They refused to give up their hold on the minds they had nourished and amused so long.

One and all the children were really distressed, with the exception of Friedrich, who had, as usual, given about half his attention to the subject in hand; and who now sat absently humming to himself the account of Bluebeard's position and character, as set forth in Gotter's ballad.

The others came to the conclusion that there was but one hope left—that St. Nicholas might have put some new ballads into the old book—and one and all they made for the hiding-place, followed at a feebler pace by the little Fräulein, who ran with her lips tightly shut, her hands clenched, and her eyes wide open with a mixture of fear and expectation. The bricks were removed, the book unwrapped, but alas! everything was the same, even to the rough woodcut of Bluebeard himself, in the act of sharpening his scimitar. There was no change, except that the volume was rather the worse for damp. It was thrown down with a murmur of disappointment, but seized immediately by the little Fräulein, who flung herself upon it in a passion of tears and embraces. Hers was the only faithful affection; the charm of the Märchen-Frau was gone.

They were all out of humour with this, and naturally looked about for some one to find fault with. Friedrich was at hand, and so they fell upon him and reproached him for his want of sympathy with their vexation. The boy awoke from a brown study, and began to defend himself:—"He was very sorry," he said; "but he couldn't see the use of making such a great fuss about a few old ballads, that after all were nothing so very wonderful."

This was flat heresy, and he was indignantly desired to say where any were to be got like them,—where even *one* might be found, when St. Nicholas could not provide them? Friedrich was even less respectful to the idea of St.

Nicholas, and said something which, translated into English, would look very like the word *humbug*. This was no answer to the question " where were they to get a ballad?" and a fresh storm came upon his head; whereupon being much goaded, and in a mixture of vanity and vexation of spirit, he let out the fact that " he thought he could write one almost as good himself."

This turned the current of affairs. The children had an instinctive belief in Friedrich's talents, to which their elders had not attained. The faith of childhood is great, and they saw no reason why he should not be able to do as he said, and so forthwith began to pet and coax him as unmercifully as they had scolded five minutes before.

" Beloved Friedrich ! dear little brother ! *Do* write one for us. We know thou canst !"

" I cannot," said Friedrich. " It is all nonsense. I was only joking."

" It is not nonsense ; we know thou canst ! Dear Fritz—just to please us !"

" Do !" said another. " It was only yesterday the mother was saying, 'Friedrich can do nothing useful !' But when thou hast written a poem thou wilt have done more than any one in the house—ay, or in the town. And when thou hast written one poem thou wilt write more, and be like Hans Sachs, and the Twelve Wise Masters thou hast told us of so often."

Friedrich had read many of the verses o the Cobbler Poet, but the name of Hans Sachs awakened no thought in his mind. He had heard nothing of that speech but one sentence, and it decided him.

Friedrich can do nothing useful. "I will see what I can do," he said, and walked hastily away. Down the garden, out into the road, away to the mill, where he could stand by the roaring water and talk aloud without being heard.

"Friedrich can do nothing useful. Yes, I will write a ballad."

He went home, got together some scraps of paper, and commenced.

In half-a-dozen days he began as many ballads, and tore them up one and all. He beat his brains for plots, and was satisfied with none. He had a fair maiden, a cruel father, a wicked sister, a handsome knight, and a castle on the Rhine; and so plunged into a love story with a moonlight meeting, an escape on horseback, pursuit, capture, despair, suicide, and a ghostly apparition that floated over the river, and wrung her hands under the castle window. It seems impossible for an author to do more for his heroine than take her out of the world, and bring her back again; but our poet was not content. He had not come himself to the sentiment of life, and felt a rough boyish disgust at the maundering griefs of his hero and heroine, who, moreover, were unpleasantly like every other hero and heroine that he had ever read of under similar circumstances; and if there was one thing more than another that Friedrich was determined to be, it was original.

He had no half hopes. With the dauntlessness of young ambition, he determined to do his very best, and that that best should be better than anything that ever had been done by any one.

Having failed with the sentimental, he tried to write something funny. Surely such child's tales as Bluebeard, Cinderella, etc., were easy enough to write. He would make a *Kindeslied* —a child's song. But he was mistaken; to write a new nursery ballad was the hardest task of all. Time after time he struggled; and, at last, one day when he had written and destroyed a longer effort than usual, he went to bed in hopeless despair.

His disappointment mingled with his dreams. He dreamt that he was in the bookseller's shop hunting among the shelves for some scraps of paper on which he had written. He could not find them, he thought, but came across the Petrarch volumes in their beautiful binding. He opened one and saw—not a word of that fair-looking Italian, but—his own ballad that he could not write, written and printed in good German character with his name on the title-page. He took it in his hands and went out of the shop, and as he did so it seemed to him, in his dream, that he had become a man. He dreamt that as he came down the steps, the people in the street gathered round him and cheered and shouted. The women held up their children to look at him; he was a Great Man! He thought that he turned back into the shop and went up to the counter. There sat the smiling little bookseller as natural as life, who smiled and bowed to him, as Friedrich had a hundred times seen him bow and smile to the bearded men who came in to purchase.

"How many have you sold of this?" said Friedrich, in his dream.

"Forty thousand!" with another smile and bow.

Forty thousand! It seemed to him that all the world must have read it. This was Fame.

He went out of the shop, through the shouting market-place, and home, where his father led him in and offered pipes and a mug of ale, as if he were the Burgomaster. He sat down, and when his mother came in rose to embrace her, and doing so knocked down the mug. Crash! it went on to the floor with a loud noise, which woke him up; and then he found himself in bed, and that he had thrown over the mug of water which he had put by his bedside to drink during the thirsty feverish hours that he lay awake.

He was not a great man, but a child.

He had not written a ballad, but broken a mug.

" Friedrich can do nothing useful."

He buried his face, and wept bitterly.

In time his tears were dried, and as it was very early he lay awake and beat his brains. He had added nothing to his former character but the breaking of a piece of crockery. Something must be done. No more funny ballads now. He would write something terrible—miserable; something that should make other people weep as he had wept. He was in a very tragic humour indeed. He would have a hero who should go into the world to seek his fortune, and come back to find his lady-love in a nunnery; but that was an old story. Well, he would turn it the other way, and put the hero into a monastery; but that wasn't new. Then he would shut both of them up, and not let them meet again till one was a monk and the other a nun, which would be grievous enough in all reason; but this was the oldest of all. Friedrich gave up love stories on the spot. It was clearly not his *forte.*

Then he thought he would have a large family of brothers and sisters, and kill them all by a plague. But besides the want of further incident, this idea did not seem to him sufficiently sad. Either from its unreality, or from their better faith, the idea of death does not possess the same gloom for the young, that it does for those older minds that have a juster sense of the value of human life, and are perhaps more heavily bound in the chains of human interests.

No; the plague story might be pathetic, but it was not miserable,—not miserable enough at any rate for Friedrich.

In truth he felt at last that every misfortune that he could invent was lost in the depths of the real sorrow which oppressed his own life, and out of this knowledge came an idea for his ballad. What a fool never to have thought of it before !

He would write the history—the miserable bitter history—of a great man born to a small way of life, whose merits should raise him from his low estate to a deserved and glorious fame ; who should toil, and strive, and struggle, and when his hopes and prayers seemed to be at last fulfilled, and the reward of his labours at hand, should awake and find that it was a dream ; that he was no nearer to Fame than ever, and that he might never reach it. Here was enough sorrow for a tragedy. The ballad should be written now.

The next day Friedrich plunged into the bookseller's shop.

" Well now, what is it?" smiled the comfortable little bookseller.

" I want some paper, please," gasped Friedrich ; " a good big bit if I may have it, and if you please I must go now. I will come and clean out the shop for you at the end of the week, but I am very busy to-day."

"The condition of the shop," said the little bookseller grandiloquently, with a wave of his hand, "yields to more important matters ; namely, to thy condition my child, which is

not of the best.   Thou art as white as this
sheet of paper, to which thou art heartily wel-
come.   I am silent, but not ignorant.   Thou
wouldst be a writer, but art not yet a philosopher, my Friedrich.   Thou art not fast-set on
thy philosophic equilibrium.   Thou hast knocked
down three books and a stool since thou hast
come in the shop.   Be calm, my child : consider
that even if truly also the fast-bound-eternally-
immutable-condition of everlastingly-varying-
circumstance—"

But by this time Friedrich was at home.

How he got through the next three days he
never knew.   He stumbled in and out of the
house with the awkwardness of an idiot, and
was so stupid in school that nothing but his pre-
vious good character saved him from a flogging.
The day before the Feast of St. Nicholas (which
was a holiday) the schoolmaster dismissed him
with the severe inquiry, if he meant to be a dunce
all his life ? and Friedrich went home with two
sentences ringing in his head—

" Do I mean to be a dunce all my life ?"

" Friedrich can do nothing useful."

To-night the ballad must be finished.

He contrived to sit up beyond his usual hour,
and escaped notice by crouching behind a large

linen chest, and there wrote and wrote till his heart beat, and his head felt as if it would split in pieces. At last the maternal care discovered that Friedrich had not bid her good night, and he was brought out of his hiding-place and sent to bed.

He took a light and went softly up the ladder into the loft, and, to his great satisfaction, found the others asleep. He said his prayers, and got into bed, but he did not put out the light; he put a box behind it to prevent its being seen, and drew out his paper and wrote. The ballad was done, but he must make a fair copy for the Märchen-Frau; and very hard work it was, in his feverish excited state, to write out a thing that was finished. He worked resolutely, however, and at last completed it with trembling hands, and pushed it under his pillow.

Then he sat up in bed, and looked round him.

Time passed, and still he sat shivering and clasping his knees, and the reason he sat so was,—because he dared not lie down.

The work was done, and the overstrained mind, no longer occupied, filled with ghastly fears and fancies. He did not dare to put out the light, and yet its faint glimmer only made the darkness more horrible. He did not dare to look behind him, though he knew that there was nothing there. He trembled at the scratching sound in the wainscot, though he knew that it was only mice. A sudden light on the window, and a distant chorus, did not make his heart beat less wildly from being nothing more alarming than two or three noisy students going home with torches. Then his light took the matter into its own hands, and first flared up with a suddenness that almost made Friedrich jump out of his skin, and then left him in total darkness. He could endure no longer, and scrambling out of bed, crossed the floor to where the warm light came up the steps of the ladder from the room beneath. There our hero crouched without daring to move, and comforted himself with the sounds of life below. But it was very wearying, and yet he dared not go back. A neighbour had "dropped in," and he could see figures passing to and fro across the kitchen.

At last his sister passed, with the light shining on her golden plaits, and he risked a low murmur of "Marie! Marie!"

She stopped an instant, and then passed on; but after a few minutes she returned, and came up the ladder with her finger on her lips, to enjoin silence. He needed no caution, being

instinctively aware that if one parental duty
could be more obvious than another to the
tradesman, it would be that of crushing such
folly as Friedrich was displaying, by timely severity. The boy crept back to bed, and Marie
came after him.

There are unheroic moments in the lives of
the greatest of men, and though when the head
is strong and clear, and there is plenty of light
and good company, it is highly satisfactory and
proper to smile condescension upon female in-
anity; there are times when it is not unpleasant
to be at the mercy of kind arms that pity without asking a reason, and in whose presence
one may be foolish without shame. And it is
not ill perhaps for some of us, whose acutely
strung minds go up with every discovery, and
down with every doubt, if we have some humble
comforter (whether woman or man) on whose
face a faithful spirit has set the seal of peace,
a face which in its very steadfastness is "as the
face of an angel."

Such a face looked down upon Friedrich,
before which fancied horrors fled; and he
wound his arms round Marie's neck, and laid
down his head, and was comfortable, if not sub-
lime.

After a dozen or so of purposeless kisses, she spoke,—

"What is it, my beloved?"

"I—I don't think I can get to sleep," said the poet.

Marie abstained from commenting on this remark, and Friedrich was silent and comfortable. So comfortable, that though he despised her opinion on such matters, he asked it in a low whisper,—"Marie, dost thou not think it would be the very best thing in the world to be a great man? To labour and labour for it, and be a great man at last?"

Marie's answer was as low, but quite decided—

"No."

"Why not, Marie?"

"It is very nice to be great, and I should love to see thee a great man, Friedrich, very well indeed, but the very best thing of all is to be good. Great men are not always happy ones, though when they are good also it is very glorious, and makes one think of the words of the poor heathen in Lycaonia,—'The gods have come down to us in the likeness of men.' But if ever thou art a great man, little brother, it will be the good and not the great things of thy life that will bring thee peace. Nay, rather, neither thy goodness nor thy greatness, but the mercy of GOD ! "

And in this opinion Marie was obstinately fixed, and Friedrich argued no more.

" I think I shall do now," said the hero at last ; " I thank thee very much, Marie."

She kissed him anew, and bade GOD bless him, and wished him good-night, and went down the ladder till her golden plaits caught again the glow of the warm kitchen, and Friedrich lost sight of her tall figure and fair face, and was alone once more.

He was better, but still he could not sleep. Wearied and vexed, he lay staring into the darkness till he heard steps upon the ladder, and became the involuntary witness of——the true St. Nicholas.

It was the mother, with a basket in her hand, and Friedrich watched her as she approached the place where all the shoes were laid out, his among them.

The children were by no means immaculate, or in any way greatly superior to other families, but the mother was tender-hearted, and had a. poor memory for sins that were past, and Friedrich saw her fill one shoe after another

H

with cakes and sweetmeats. At last she came to
his, and then she stopped. He lifted up his head,
and an indefinable fury surged in his heart. He
had been very tiresome since the ballad was
begun; was she going to put rods into his shoes
only? *His!* He could have borne anything
but this. Meanwhile, she was fumbling in the
basket; and, at last, pulled out—not a rod,
but—a paper of cakes of another kind, to which
Friedrich was particularly attached, and with
these she lined the shoes thickly, and filled
them up with sweetmeats, and passed on.

"Oh, mother! mother! Far, far too kind !"
The awkwardness and stupidity of yesterday,
and of many yesterdays, smote him to the
heart, and roused once more the only too ready
tears. But he did not cry long, he had a happy
feeling of community with his brothers and
sisters in getting more than they any of them
deserved; it was quite what English boys would
call "a lark" to have seen the St. Nicholas's
proceedings, and altogether, with a comfortable
sensation of cakes and kindness, he fell asleep
smiling, and slept soundly and well.

The next day he threw his arms round his
mother, and said that the cakes were "so nice."

"But I don't deserve them," he added.

"Thou'lt mend," said she kindly. "And no doubt the Saint knew that thou hadst eaten but a half a dinner for a week past, and brought those cakes to tempt thee; so eat them all, my child; for, doubtless, there are plenty more where they come from."

"I am very much obliged to whomever did think of it," said Friedrich.

"And plenty more there are," said the good woman to Marie afterwards, as they were dishing the dinner. "Luise Jansen's shop is full of them. But bless the boy! he's too sharp for anything. There's no coming St. Nicholas over him."

The day went by at last, and the evening came on. The tradesman went off of himself to see if he could meet with the Burgomaster, and the children became rabid in their impatience for Friedrich's ballad.

He would not read it himself, so Marie was pressed into the service, and crowned with the hood and cloak, and elected Märchen-Frau.

The author himself sat in an arm-chair, with a face as white and miserable as if he were ordered for execution. He formed a painful contrast to his ruddy brothers and sisters; and it would seem as if he had begun already to experience the truth of Marie's assertion, that " great men are not always happy ones."

The ballad was put into the Märchen-Frau's hands, and she was told that Friedrich had written it. She gave a quick glance at it, and asked if he had really invented it all. The children repeated the fact, which was a pleasant but not a surprising one to them, and Marie began.

The young poet had evidently a good ear, for the verses were easy and musical, and the metre more than tolerably correct; and as the hero of the ballad worked harder and harder, and got higher and higher, the children clapped their hands, and discovered that it was "quite like Friedrich."

Why, when that hero was almost at the height of fortune, and the others gloried in his success, did the foolish author bury his face upon his arms, and sob silently but bitterly in sympathy?—moreover, with such a heavy and absorbing grief that he did not hear it, when Marie stopped for an instant and then went on again, or know that steps had come behind his chair, and that his father and the Burgomaster were in the room.

The Märchen-Frau went on; the hero awoke from his unreal happiness to his real fate, and bewailed in verse after verse the heavy weights of birth, and poverty, and circumstance, that kept him from the heights of fame. The ballad was ended.

Then a voice fell on Friedrich's ear, which nearly took away his breath. It was his father's, asking sternly, " What is all this ? "

And then he knew that Marie was standing up, with a strange emotion on her face, and he heard her say,

" It is a poem that Friedrich has written. He has written it all himself. Every word. And he is but twelve years old ! " She was pointing to him, or, perhaps, the Burgomaster might not have recognized in that huddled miserable figure the Genius of the family.

His was the next voice, and what he said Friedrich could hardly remember; the last sentences only he clearly understood.

" God has not blessed me with children, neighbour. My wife, as well as I, would be ashamed if such genius were lost for want of a little money. Give the child to me. He shall have a liberal education, and will be a great man."

"I shall not," said the tradesman, "stand in the way of his interests or your commands. I cannot tell what to say to your kindness, Burgomaster. GOD willing, I hope he will be a credit to the town."

"GOD willing, he will be a credit to his country," said the Burgomaster.

The words rang in Friedrich's ears over and over again, like the changes of bells. They danced before his eyes as if he saw them in a book. They were written in his heart as if "graven with an iron pen and lead in the rock for ever."

"GOD *willing, I hope he will be a credit to the town.*"

"GOD *willing, he will be a credit to his country.*"

"*He shall have a liberal education, and will be a* GREAT MAN."

Friedrich tried to stand on his feet and thank the Burgomaster; who, on any other occasion, might have been tempted to suppose him an idiot, so white and distorted was the child's face, struggling through tears and smiles. He could not utter a word; a mist began to come before his eyes, through which the Burgomaster's head seemed to bob up and down, and then his father's and his mother's, and Marie's, with a look of pity on her face. He tried to tell *her* that he was now a great man and felt quite happy; but, unfortunately, was only able to burst into tears, and then to burst out laughing, and then a sharp pain shot through his head, and he remembered no more.

Friedrich had a dim consciousness of coming round after this, and being put to bed; then he fell asleep, and slept heavily. When he woke Marie was sitting by his side, and it was dark. The mother had gone downstairs, she said, and she had taken her place. Friedrich lay silent for a bit; at last he said,

"I am very happy, Marie."

"I am very glad, dearest."

"Dost thou think father will let the Burgomaster give me a good education, Marie?"

"Yes, dear, I am sure he will."

"It is very kind," said Friedrich thoughtfully; "for I know he wants me for the business. But I will help him some day. And Marie, I will be a good man, and when I am very rich I will give great alms to the poor."

"Thou wilt be a good man before thou art a rich one, I trust," said his dogmatic sister. "We are accepted in that we have, and not in that we have not. Thou hast great talent, and wilt give it to the Lord, whether He make thee rich or no. Wilt thou not, dearest?"

"What dost thou mean, Marie? Am I never to write anything but hymns?"

"No, no, I do not mean that," she said. "I am very ignorant, and cannot rightly explain it to thee, little brother. But genius is a great and perilous gift; and, oh, Friedrich! Friedrich! promise me just this:—that thou wilt never, never write anything against the faith or the teaching of the Saviour, and that thou wilt never use the graces of poetry to cover the hideousness of any of those sins which it is the work of a lifetime to see justly, and to fight against manfully. Promise me just this."

"Oh, Marie! To think that I could be so wicked!"

"No! no!" she said, covering him with kisses. "I know thou wilt be good and great, and we shall all be proud of our little brother. God give thee the pen of a ready writer, and grace to use it to His glory!"

"I will," he said, "God help me! and I will write beautiful hymns for thee, Marie, that when I am dead shall be sung in the churches.

They shall be like that Evening Hymn we sing so often. Sing it now, my sister!"

Marie cleared her throat, and in a low voice, that steadied and grew louder and sweeter till it filled the house and died away among the rafters, sang the beautiful old hymn that begins

"Herr, Dein Auge geht nicht unter, wenn es bei uns Abend wird;"

(Lord! Thine eye does not go down when it is evening with us.)

The boy lay drinking it in with that full enjoyment of simple vocal music which is so innate in the German character; and as he lay he hummed his accustomed part in it, and the mother at work below caught up the song involuntarily, and sang at her work; and Marie's clear voice breaking through the wooden walls of the house, was heard by a passer in the street, who struck in with the bass of the familiar hymn, and went his way. Before it was ended, Friedrich was sleeping peacefully once more.

But Marie sat by the stove till the watchman in the quaint old street told the hour of midnight, when (with the childish custom taught her by the old schoolmaster long ago) she folded her hands, and murmured,

"Nisi Dominus urbem custodiat, frustra vigilat custos."

(Except the Lord keep the city, the watchman waketh but in vain.)

And then she slept also.

The snow fell softly on the roof, and on the walls of the old church outside, and on the pavement of the street of the poet's native town, and the night passed and the day came.

There is little more to tell, for that night was the last night of his sorrowful humble childhood, and that day was the first day of his fame.

.   .   .   .   .

The Duke of —— was an enlightened and generous man, and a munificent patron of the Arts and Sciences, and of literary and scientific men. He was not exactly a genius, but he was highly accomplished. He wrote a little, and played a little, and drew a little; and with Fortune to befriend him, as a natural consequence he published a little, and composed a little, and framed his pictures.

But what was better and more remarkable than this, was the generous spirit in which he loved and admired those who did great things in the particular directions in which he did a little. He bought good pictures while he painted bad ones; and those writers, musicians, and artists who could say but little for his performances, had every reason to talk loudly of his liberality. He was the special admirer of talent born in obscurity; and at the time of which we are writing (many years after the events related above), the favourite "lion" in the literary clique he had gathered round him in his palace, was a certain poet,—the son of a small tradesman in a small town, who had been educated by the kindness of the Burgomaster (long dead), and who now had made Germany to ring with his fame;—who had visited the Courts of Europe, and received compliments from Royalty, whose plays were acted in the theatres, whose poems stood on the shelves of the booksellers, who was a great man—Friedrich!

It was a lovely evening, and the Duke, leaning on the arm of his favourite, walked up and down a terrace. The Duke was (as usual) in the best possible humour. The poet (as was not uncommon) was just in the slightest degree inclined to be in a bad one. They had been reading a critique on his poems. It was praise it is true, but the praise was not judiciously administered, and the poet was aggrieved. He

rather felt (as authors are not unapt to feel)
that a poet who could write such poems should
have critics created with express capabilities
for understanding him. But the good Duke
was in his most cheery and amiable mood, and
quite bent upon smoothing his ruffled lion into
the same condition.

" What impossible creatures you geniuses are
to please ! " he said. " Tell me, my friend, has
there ever been, since you first began your
career, a bit of homage or approbation that has
really pleased you ? "

" Oh yes ! " said the poet, in a tone that
sounded like Oh no !

" I don't believe it," said the Duke. " Come,
now, could you, if you were asked, describe the
happiest and proudest hour of your life ? "

A new expression came into the poet's eyes,
and lighted up his gaunt intellectual face. Some
old memories awoke within him, and it is doubtful if he saw the landscape at which he was
gazing. But the Duke was not quick, though
kind ; he thought that Friedrich had not heard
him, and repeated the question.

" Yes," said the poet. " Yes, indeed I
could."

" Well, then, let me guess," said the Duke

facetiously. (He fancied that he was bringing his crusty genius into capital condition.) "Was it when your great tragedy of 'Boadicea' was first performed in Berlin, and the theatre rose like one man to offer homage, and the gods sent thunder? I wish they had ever treated my humble efforts with as much favour. Was it then?"

"No!"

"Was it when his Imperial Majesty the Emperor of —— was pleased to present you with a gold snuff-box set with diamonds, and to express his opinion that your historical plays were incomparably among the finest productions of poetic genius?"

"His Imperial Majesty," said Friedrich, "is a brave soldier; but, a—ahem!—an indifferent critic. I do not take snuff, and his Imperial Majesty does not read poetry. The interview was gratifying, but that was not the occasion. No!"

"Was it when you were staying with Dr. Kranz at G——, and the students made that great supper for you, and escorted your carriage both ways with a procession of torches?"

"Poor boys!" said the poet, laughing; "it was very kind, and they. could ill afford it.

But they would have drunk quite as much wine
for any one who would have taken the inside
out of the University clock, or burnt the Principal's wig, as they did for me. It was a very
unsteady procession that brought me home, I
assure you. The way they poked the torches
in each other's faces left one student, as I
heard, with no less than eight duels on his
hands. And oh! the manner in which they
howled my most pathetic love songs! No!
no!"

The Duke laughed heartily.

" Is it any of the various occasions on which
the fair ladies of Germany have testified their
admiration by offerings of sympathy and handi-
work?"

"No!" roared the poet.

" Are you quite sure?" said the Duke slyly.
" I have heard of comforters, and slippers, and
bouquets, and locks of hair, besides a dozen of
warm stockings knit by the fair hands of——"

" Spare me!" groaned Friedrich, in mock
indignation. "Am I a pet preacher, that I
should be smothered in female absurdities? I
have hair that would stuff a sofa, comforters
that would protect a regiment in Siberia, slippers, stockings——. I shall sell them, I shall

burn them. I would send them back, but the
ladies send nothing but their Christian names,
and to identify Luise, and Gretchen, and Cathe-
rine, and Bettina, is beyond my powers. No!"

When they had ceased laughing the Duke
continued his catechism..

"Was it when the great poet G—— (your
only rival) paid that handsome compliment to
your verses on—"

"No!" interrupted the poet. "A thousand
times no! The great poet praised the verses
you allude to simply to cover his depreciation
of my 'Captive Queen,' which is among my
best efforts, but too much in his own style.
How Germany can worship his bombastic——
but that's nothing! No."

"Was it when you passed accidentally through
the streets of Dresden, and the crowd discovered you, and carried you to the hotel on its
shoulders?"

The momentary frown passed from Friedrich's
face, and he laughed again.

"And when the men who carried me twisted
my leg so that I couldn't walk for a fortnight,
to say nothing of the headache I endured from
bowing to the populace like a Chinese man-
darin? No!"

" Is it any triumph you have enjoyed in any other country in Europe ? "

" No ! "

" My dear genius, I can guess no more; what, in the name of Fortune, was this happy occasion—this life triumph ? "

" It is a long story, your highness, and entertaining to no one but myself."

" You do me injustice," said the Duke. " A long story from you is too good to be lost. Sit down, and favour me."

A patron's wishes are not to be neglected; and somewhat unwillingly the poet at last sat down, and told the story of his Ballad and of St. Nicholas's Day, as it has been told here. The fountain of tears is drier in middle age than in childhood, but he was not unmoved as he concluded.

" Every circumstance of that evening," he said, " is as fresh in my remembrance now as it was then, and will be till I die. It is a joy, a triumph, and a satisfaction that will never fade. The words that roused me from despair, that promised knowledge to my ignorance and fame to my humble condition, have power now to make my heart beat, and to bring hopeful tears into eyes that should have dried with age—

"God *willing, he will be a credit to the town.*

"God *willing, he will be a credit to his country.*

"*He shall have a liberal education, and will be a great man.*"

"It is as good as a poem," said the delighted Duke. "I shall tell the company tonight that I am the most fortunate man in Germany. I have heard your unpublished poem. By the bye, Poet, is that ballad published?"

"No, and never will be. It shall never know less kindly criticism than it received then."

"And are you really in earnest? Was this indeed the happiest triumph your talents have ever earned?"

"It was," said Friedrich. "The first blast on the trumpet of Fame is the sweetest. Afterwards, we find it out of tune."

"Your parents are dead, I think?"

"They are, and so is my youngest sister."

"And what of Marie?"

"She married,—a man who, I think, is in no way worthy of her. Not a bad, but a stupid man, with strong Bible convictions on the subject of marital authority. She is such an angel in his house as he can never understand in this world."

I

" Do you ever see her ? "

" Sometimes, when I want a rest. I went to
see her not long ago, and found her just the same
as ever. I sat at her feet, and laid my head in
her lap, and tried to be a child again. I bade her
tell me the history of Bluebeard, and strove to
forget that I had ever lost the childish simplicity which she has kept so well ;—and I almost succeeded. I had forgotten that the great
poet was jealous of my ' Captive Queen,' and told
myself it would be a grand thing to be like
him. I thought I should like to see a live
Emperor. But just when the delusion was perfect, there was a row in the street. The people
had found me out, and I must show myself at
the window. The spell was broken. I have
not tried it again."

They were on the steps of the palace.

" Your story has entertained and touched me
beyond measure," said the Duke. " But something is wanting. It does not (as they say)
' end well.' I fear you are not happy."

" I am content," said Friedrich. " Yes, I am
happy. I never could be a child again, even if
it pleased GOD to restore to me the circumstances of my childhood. It is best as it is,
but I have learnt the truth of what Marie told

me. It is the good, and not the great things of my life that bring me peace; or, rather, neither one nor the other, but the undeserved mercies of my GOD!"

.   .   .   .   .

For those who desire to know more of the poet's life than has been told, this is added. He did not live to be very old. A painful disease (the result of mental toil), borne through many years, ended his life almost in its prime. He retained his faculties till the last, and bore protracted suffering with a heroism and endurance, which he had not always displayed in smaller trials. The medical men pronounced, on the authority of a *post-mortem* examination, that he must for years have suffered a silent martyrdom. Truly his bodily sufferings (when known at last) might well excuse many weaknesses, and much moody irritable impatience; especially when it is remembered that the mental sufferings of intellectual men are generally great in proportion to their gifts; and (when clogged with nerves and body that are ever urged beyond their strength) that they often mock the pride of humanity by leaving but little space between the genius and the madman.

Another fact was not known till he had died— his charity. Then it was discovered how much kindness he had exercised in secret, and that three poor widows had been fed daily from his table during all the best years of his prosperity. Before his death he arranged all his affairs, even to the disposal of his worn-out body.

"My country has been gracious to me," he said, "and if it cares, may dispose of my carcase as it will. But I desire that after my death my heart may be taken from my body, and buried at the feet of my father and my mother in the churchyard of my native town. At their feet," he added, with some of the old imperiousness—'strong in death.' "At their feet, remember!"

In one of the largest cities of Germany, a huge marble monument is erected to the memory of the Great Man. On three sides of the pedestal are bas-relief designs illustrating some of his works, whereby three fellow-countrymen added to their fame; and on the fourth is a fine inscription in Latin, setting forth his talents, and his virtues, and the honours conferred on him, and stating in conclusion (on the authority of his eulogizer) that his works have gained for him immortality.

In a quiet green churchyard, near a quiet little town, under the shadow of the quaint old church, a little cross marks the graves of a tradesman and of his wife who lived and laboured in their generation, and are at rest. Near them daisies grow above the dust of the "Fräulein' which awaits the resurrection from the dead. And at the feet of that simple couple lies the heart of their great son—a heart which the sickness of earthly hope, and the fever of earthly ambition, shall disturb no more.

By the Poet's own desire the "rude memorial" that marks the spot contains no more than his initials, and a few words in his native tongue, to mark the foundation of the only ambition that he could feel in death—

"Ich verlasse mich auf Gottes Güte immer und ewiglich."

—*My trust is in the tender mercy of* God *for ever and ever.*

A BIT OF GREEN.

"Thou oughtest therefore to call to mind the more heavy
sufferings of others, that so thou mayest the easier bear thy
own very small troubles."—THE IMITATION OF CHRIST.

CHILDREN who live always with grass and
flowers at their feet, and a clear sky overhead,
can have no real idea of the charm that country
sights and sounds have for those whose home
is in a dirty, busy, manufacturing town,—just
such a town, in fact, as I lived in when I was a
boy, which is more than twenty years ago.

My father was a doctor, with a very large, if
not what is called a "genteel" practice, and we
lived in a comfortable house in a broad street.
I was born and bred there; and ever since I
could remember, the last sound that .soothed
my ears at night, and the first to which I
awoke in the morning, was the eternal rumbling
and rattling of the carts and carriages as they
passed over the rough stones. I never noticed
if I heard them in the day-time; but at night
my chief amusement, as I lay in bed, was to

A BIT OF GREEN.

guess by the sound of the wheels what sort of vehicle was passing.

"That light sharp rattle is a cab," I thought; "what a noise it makes, and gone in a moment! one gentleman inside, I should think; there's an omnibus; and there, jolty-jolt, goes a light cart; that's a carriage, by the way the horses step; and now, rumbling heavily in the distance, and coming slowly nearer, and heavier, and louder—this can be nothing but a brewer's dray!" And the dray came so slowly, that I was asleep before it had got safely out of hearing. Ours was a very noisy street, but the noise made the night cheerful; and so did the church clock near, which struck the quarters; and so did the light of the street lamps, which came through the blind and fell upon my little bed. We had very little light, except gaslight and daylight, in our street; the sunshine seldom found its way to us; and when it did, people were so little used to it that they pulled down the blinds for fear it should hurt the carpets. In the room my sister and I called our nursery, however, we always welcomed it with blinds rolled up to the very top; and as we had no carpet, no damage was done.

But sunshine outside will not always make

sunshine within; and I remember one day
when, though our nursery was unusually cheerful, and though the windows were reflected in
square patches of sunlight on the floor, I stood
in the very midst of the brightness, grumbling
and kicking at my sister's chair, with a face
as black as a thunder-cloud. The reason of
my ill-temper was this: Ever since I could remember, my father had been accustomed, once
a year, to take us all into the country for
change of air. Once he had taken us to the
sea: but generally we went to an old farm-
house in the middle of the beautiful moors
which lay not many miles from our dirty black
town. But this year, on this very sunshiny
morning, he had announced at breakfast that
he could not let us go to what we called our
moor-home. He had even added insult to in-
jury, by expressing his thankfulness that we were
all in good health, and so that the change was
not a matter of necessity. I was too indignant
to speak, and rushed upstairs into the nursery,
where my little sister had also taken refuge.
She was always very gentle and obedient, (pro-
vokingly so, I thought!) and now she sat rocking her doll on her knee in silent sorrow, whilst
I stook kicking her chair, and grumbling in

a tone which it was well the doll could not hear, or rocking would have been of little use. I took pleasure in trying to make her as angry as myself. I reminded her how lovely the purple moors were looking at that moment, how sweet heather smelt, and how good bilberries tasted. I said I thought it was " very hard." It wasn't as if we were always paying visits, as many children did to their country relations; we had only one treat in the year, and father wanted to take that away. Not a soul in the town, I said, would be as unfortunate as we were. The children next-door would go somewhere, of course. So would the little Smiths, and the Browns, and *everybody.* Everybody else went to the sea in the autumn ; we were contented with the moors, and he wouldn't even let us go there. And at the end of every burst of complaint, I discharged a volley of kicks at the leg of the chair, and wound up with " I can't think why he can't ! ".

" I don't know," said my sister timidly, " but he said something about not affording it, and spending money, and about trade being bad, and he was afraid there would be great distress in the town."

Oh, these illogical women ! I was furious.

"What on earth has that to do with us?" I shouted at her. "Father's a doctor; trade won't hurt him. But you are so silly, Minnie, I can't talk to you. I only know it's very hard. Fancy staying a whole year boxed up in this beastly town!" And I had so worked myself up, that I fully believed in the truth of the sentence with which I concluded,

"*There never* WAS *anything so miserable!*"

Minnie said nothing, for my feelings just then were something like those of the dogs who (Dr. Watts tells us)

"delight
To bark and bite;"

and perhaps she was afraid of being bitten. At any rate, she held her tongue; and just then my father came into the room.

The door was open, and he must have heard my last speech as he came along the passage; but he made no remark on it, and only said, "Would any young man here like to go with me to see a patient?"

I went willingly, for I was both tired and half ashamed of teasing Minnie; and we were soon in the street. It was a broad and cheerful one as I said; but before long we left it for a narrower, and then turned off from that into a side street, where the foot-path would only allow us to walk in single file—a dirty dark lane, where surely the sun never did shine.

" What a horrid place ! " I said ; " I never was here before. Why don't they pull such a street down ? "

" What is to become of the people who live in it ? " said my father.

" Let them live in one of the bigger streets," I said ; " it would be much more comfortable."

" Very likely," he said ; " but they would have to pay much more for their houses ; and if they haven't the money to pay with, what's to be done ? "

I could not say ; for, like older social reformers than myself, I felt more sure that the reform was needed, than of how to accomplish it. But before I could decide upon what to do with the dirty little street, we had come to a place so very much worse that it put the other quite out of my head. There is a mournful fatality about the pretty names which are given, as if in mockery, to the most wretched of the bye-streets in large towns. The street we had left was called Rosemary Street, and this was Primrose Place.

Primrose Place was more like a yard than

a street; the houses were all irregular and of
different ages; on one side was a gap with
palings round it, where building was going
on; and beyond rose a huge black factory.
But the condition of Primrose Place was beyond description. I had never seen anything
like it before, and kept as close to my father
as was consistent with boyish dignity. The
pathway was broken up, children squalled at
the doors and quarrelled in the street, which
was strewn with rags, and bones, and bits of
old iron, and shoes, and the tops of turnips.
I do not think there was a whole unbroken
window in all the row of tall miserable houses;
and the wet clothes hanging out on lines
stretched across the street, flapped above our
heads. I counted three cripples as we went
up Primrose Place. My father stopped to
speak to several people, and I heard many com-
plaints of the bad state of trade to which my
sister had alluded. He gave some money to
one woman, and spoke kindly to all; but he
hurried me on as fast as he could, and we
turned at last into one of the houses.

My ill-humour had by this time almost
worked itself off in the fresh air, and the novel
scenes through which we had come; and for

the present the morning's disappointment was
forgotten, as I followed my father through the
crowded miserable rooms, and clambered up
staircase after staircase, till we reached the top
of the house, and stumbled through a latched
door into the garret. After so much groping
in the dark, the light dazzled me, and I thought
at first that the room was empty. But at last
a faint "Good day" from the corner near the
window drew my eyes that way; and there,
stretched on a sort of bed, and supported by a
chair at his back, lay the patient we had come
to see.

He was a young man about twenty-six years
old, in the last stage of that terrible disease so
fatally common in our country—he was dying
of consumption. There was no mistaking the
flushed cheek, the painfully laborious breathing,
and the incessant cough; while two old crutches
in the corner spoke of another affliction—he
was a cripple. His gaunt face lighted up with
a glow of pleasure when my father came in,
who seated himself at once on the end of the
bed, and began to talk to him, whilst I looked
round the room. There was absolutely nothing
in it, except the bed on which the sick man lay,
the chair that supported him, and a small three-

legged table. The low roof was terribly out of
repair, and the window was patched with news-
paper; but through the glass panes that were
left, in full glory streamed the sun, and in the
midst of the blaze stood a pot of musk in full
bloom. The soft yellow flowers looked so grand,
and smelled so sweet, that I was lost in admiration, till I found the sick man's black eyes
fixed on mine.

"You are looking at my bit of green,
Master?" he said in a gratified tone.

"Do you like flowers?" I inquired, coming
shyly up to the bed.

"Do I like 'em?" he exclaimed in a low
voice. "Ay, I love 'em well enough—well
enough," and he looked fondly at the plant,
"though it's long since I saw any but these."

"You have not been in the country for a
long time?" I inquired compassionately. I
felt sad to think that he had perhaps lain there
for months, without a taste of fresh air or a
run in the fields; but I was *not* prepared for his
answer.

"*I never was in the country, young gentleman.*"

I looked at my father.

"Yes," he said, in answer to my glance, "it

is quite true. William was born here. He got hurt when a boy, and has been lame ever since. For some years he has been entirely confined to the house. He was never out of town, and never saw a green field."

Never out of the town! confined to the house for years! and what a house! The tears rushed to my eyes, and I felt that angry heart-ache which the sight of suffering produces in those who are too young to be insensible to it, and too ignorant of GOD's Providence to submit with "quietness and confidence" to His will.

"My son can hardly believe it, William."

"It is such a shame," I said; "it is horrible. I am very sorry for you."

The black eyes turned kindly upon me, and the sick man said, "Thank you heartily, Sir. You mean very kindly. I used to say the same sort of things myself, when I was younger, and knew no better. I used to think it was very hard, and that no one was so miserable as I was. But I know now how much better off I am than most folks, and how many things I have to be thankful for."

I looked round the room, and began involuntarily to count the furniture—one, two, three. The "many things" were certainly not chairs and tables.

But he was gazing before him, and went on :
"I often think how thankful I ought to be to
die in peace, and have a quiet room to myself.
There was a girl in a consumption on the floor
below me; and she used to sit and cough, while
her father and mother quarrelled so that I could
hear them through the floor. I used to send
her half of anything nice I had, but I found
they took it. I did wish then," he added, with
a sudden flush, "that I had been a strong man."

"How shocking !" I said.

"Yes," he answered; "it was that first set
me thinking how many mercies I had. And
then there came such a good parson to St.
John's, and he taught me many things; and
then I knew your father; and the neighbours
have been very kind. And while I could work
I got good wage, and laid by a bit; and I've
sold a few things, and there'll be these to sell
when I'm gone; and so I've got what will keep
me while I do live, and pay for my coffin.
What can a man want more ?"

What, indeed ! Unsatisfied heart, make
answer !

A fit of coughing that shook the crazy room
interrupted him here. When he had recovered
himself, he turned to my father.

" Ay, ay, I have many mercies, as you know, Sir. Who would have thought I could have kept a bit of green like that plant of mine in a place like this? But, you see, they pulled down those old houses opposite just before I got it, and now the sun couldn't come into a king's room better than it comes into mine. I was always afraid, year after year, that they would build it up, and my bit of green would die : and they are building now, but it will last my time. Indeed, indeed, I've had much to be thankful for. Not," he added in a low, reverential tone, " not to mention greater blessings. The presence of the LORD ! the presence of the LORD !"

I was awed, almost frightened, by the tone in which he spoke, and by the look of his face, on which the shadow of death was falling fast. He lay in a sort of stupor, gazing with his black eyes at the broken roof, as if through it he saw something invisible to us.

It was some time before he seemed to recollect that we were there, and before I ventured to ask him, " Where did you get your plant ?"

He smiled. " That's a long story, master; but it was this way. You see, my father died quite young in a decline, and left my mother

K

to struggle on with eight of us as she could. She buried six, one after another; and then she died herself, and brother Ben and I were left alone. But we were mighty fond of one another, and got on very well. I got plenty of employment, weaving mats and baskets for a shop in the town, and Ben worked at the factory. One Saturday night he came home all in a state, and said there was going to be a cheap trip on the Monday into the country. It was the first there had been from these parts, though there have been many since, I believe. Neither he nor I had ever been out of the town, and he was full of it that we must go. He had brought his Saturday's wage with him, and we would work hard afterwards. Well, you see, the landlord had been that day, and had said he must have the rent by Tuesday, or he'd turn us out. I'd got some of it laid by, and was looking to Ben's wages to make it up. But I couldn't bear to see his face pining for a bit of fresh air, and so I thought I could stay at home and work on Monday for what would make up the rent, and he need never know. So I pretended that I didn't want to go, and couldn't be bothered with the fuss; and at last I set him off on Monday without me. It was late at

night when he came back like one wild. He'd
got flowers in his hat, and flowers in all his
button-holes; he'd got his handkerchief filled
with hay, and was carrying something under
his coat. He began laughing and crying, and
'Eh, Bill!' he said, ' thou hast been a fool. Thou
hast missed summat. But I've brought thee
a bit of green, lad, I've brought thee a bit of
green.' And then he lift up his coat, and there
was the plant, which some woman had given
him. We didn't sleep much that night. He
spread the hay over the bed, for me to lay my
face on, and see how the fields smelt, and then
he began and told me all about it; and after
that, when I was tired with work, or on a Sunday afternoon, I used to say, ' Now, Ben, tell
us a bit about the country.' And he liked nothing better. He used to say that I should go,
if he carried me on his back ; but the LORD did
not see fit. He took cold at work, and went
off three months afterwards. It was singular,
the morning he died he called me to him, and
said, ' Bill, I've been a dreaming about that
trip, that thou didst want to go after all. I
dreamt——' and then he stopped, and said no
more; but, after a bit, he opened his eyes
wide, and pulled me to him, and he said, ' Bill,

my lad, there's such flowers in heaven, such
flowers!' And so the LORD took him. But I
kept the bit of green for his sake."

Here followed another fit of coughing, which
brought my father from the end of the bed to
forbid his talking any more.

"I have got to see another patient in the
yard," he said, "and I will leave my son here.
He shall read you a chapter or two till I come
back; he is a good reader for his age."

And so my father went. I was, as he said, a
good reader for my age; but I felt very nervous
when the sick man drew a Bible from his side,
and put it in my hands. I wondered what I
should read; but it was soon settled by his
asking for certain Psalms, which I read as
clearly and distinctly as I could. At first I
was rather disturbed by his occasional remarks,
and a few murmured Amens; but I soon got
used to it. He joined devoutly in the "Glory
be to the Father"—with which I concluded—
and then asked for a chapter from the Revelation of St. John. I was more at ease now, and
read my best, with a happy sense of being useful; whilst he lay in the sunshine, folding the
sheet with his bony fingers, with his eyes fixed
on the beloved "bit of green," and drinking in
the Words of Life with dying ears.

" Blessed are they that dwell in the heavenly Jerusalem, where there is no need of the sun, neither of the moon, to shine in it ; for the glory of GOD *does lighten it, and the Lamb is the light thereof."*

By the time that my father returned, the sick man and I were fast friends; and I left him with his blessing on my head. As we went home, my good kind father told me that I was nearly old enough now to take an interest in his concerns, and began to talk of his patients, and of the poverty and destitution of some parts of the town. Then he spoke of the bad state of trade—that it was expected to be worse, and that the want of work and consequent misery this year would probably be very great. Finally he added, that when so many were likely to be starving, he had thought it right that we should deny ourselves our little annual treat, and so save the money to enable us to take our part in relieving the distressed.

"Don't you think so, my boy?" he concluded, as we reached the door of our comfortable (how comfortable!) home.

My whole heart was in my "Yes."

It is a happy moment for a son when his father first confides in him. It is a happy moment for a father when his son first learns to appreciate some of the labour of his life, and henceforth to obey his commands, not only with a blind obedience, but in the sympathizing spirit of the "perfect love" which "casts out fear." My heart was too full to thank him then for his wise forbearance, and wiser confidence; but when after some months my sister's health made change of air to the house of a country relative necessary, great was my pride and thankfulness that I was well enough to remain at the post of duty by my father's side.

One day, not long after our visit to William, he went again to see him; and when he came back I saw by the musk-plant in his hand the news he brought. Its flowers were lovelier than ever, but its master was transplanted into a heavenly garden, and he had left it to me.

Mortal man does not learn any virtue in one lesson; and I have only too often in my life been ungrateful both to GOD and man. But the memory of lame William has often come across me when I have been tempted to grumble about small troubles; and has given me a little help (not to be despised) in striving after the grace of Thankfulness, even for a "bit of green."

THE PRISONER OF THE ABBAYE.

MONSIEUR THE VISCOUNT'S FRIEND.

A TALE IN THREE CHAPTERS.

" Sweet are the vses of aduersitie
Which like the toad, ougly and venemous,
Weares yet a precious Iewell in his head."
As You Like It: A.D. 1623.

CHAPTER I.

It was the year of grace 1779. In one of the
most beautiful corners of beautiful France stood
a grand old château. It was a fine old building,
with countless windows large and small, with
high pitched roofs and pointed towers, which,
in good taste or bad, did its best to be every-
where ornamental, from the gorgon heads which
frowned from its turrets to the long row of
stables and the fantastic dovecotes. It stood (as
became such a castle) upon an eminence, and
looked down. Very beautiful indeed was what it
looked upon. Terrace below terrace glowed with
the most brilliant flowers, and broad flights of

steps led from one garden to the other. On the last terrace of all, fountains and jets of water poured into one large basin, in which were gold and silver fish. Beyond this were shady walks, which led to a lake on which floated water-lilies and swans. From the top of the topmost flight of steps you could see the blazing gardens one below the. other, the fountains and the basin, the walks and the lake, and beyond these the trees, and the smiling country, and the blue sky of France.

Within the castle, as without, beauty reigned supreme. The sunlight, subdued by blinds and curtains, stole into rooms furnished with every grace and luxury that could be procured in a country that then accounted itself the most highly-civilized in the world. It fell upon beautiful flowers and beautiful china, upon beautiful tapestry and pictures; and it fell upon Madame the Viscountess, sitting at her embroidery. Madame the Viscountess was not young, but she was not the least beautiful object in those stately rooms. She had married into a race of nobles who (themselves famed for personal beauty) had been scrupulous in the choice of lovely wives. The late Viscount (for Madame was a widow) had been one of the handsomest of the gay

courtiers of his day; and Madame had not been
unworthy of him. Even now, though the roses
on her cheeks were more entirely artificial than
they had been in the days of her youth, she was
like some exquisite piece of porcelain. Standing
by the embroidery frame was Madame's only
child, a boy who, in spite of his youth, was
already Monsieur the Viscount. He also was
beautiful. His exquisitely-cut mouth had a curl
which was the inheritance of scornful genera-
tions, but which was redeemed by his soft violet
eyes and by natural amiability reflected on his
face. His hair was cut square across the forehead, and fell in natural curls behind. His
childish figure had already been trained in the
fencing school, and had gathered dignity from
perpetually treading upon shallow steps and in
lofty rooms. From the rosettes on his little
shoes to his *chapeau à plumes*, he also was like
some porcelain figure. Surely, such beings
could not exist except in such a château as this,
where the very air (unlike that breathed by
common mortals) had in the ante-rooms a faint
aristocratic odour, and was for yards round
Madame the Viscountess dimly suggestive of
frangipani !

Monsieur the Viscount did not stay long by

the embroidery frame; he was entertaining to-day a party of children from the estate, and had come for the key of an old cabinet of which he wished to display the treasures. When tired of this, they went out on to the terrace, and one of the children who had not been there before exclaimed at the beauty of the view.

"It is true," said the little Viscount, carelessly, "and all, as far as you can see, is the estate."

"I will throw a stone to the end of your pro-perty, Monsieur," said one of the boys, laugh-ing; and he picked one off the walk, and stepping back, flung it with all his little strength. The stone fell before it had passed the fountains, and the failure was received with shouts of laughter.

"Let us see who can beat that," they cried; and there was a general search for pebbles, which were flung at random among the flower-beds.

"One may easily throw such as those," said the Viscount, who was poking under the wall of the first terrace; "but here is a stone that one may call a stone. Who will send this into the fish-pond? It will make a fountain of itself."

The children drew round him as, with ruffles turned back, he tugged and pulled at a large dirty-looking stone, which was half-buried in the earth by the wall. "Up it comes!" said the Viscount, at length; and sure enough, up it came; but underneath it, his bright eyes shining out of his dirty wrinkled body—horror of horrors!—there lay a toad. Now, even in England, toads are not looked upon with much favour, and a party of English children would have been startled by such a discovery. But with French people, the dread of toads is ludicrous in its intensity. In France toads are believed to have teeth, to bite, and to spit poison; so my hero and his young guests must be excused for taking flight at once with a cry of dismay. On the next terrace, however, they paused, and seeing no signs of the enemy, crept slowly back again. The little Viscount (be it said) began to feel ashamed of himself, and led the way, with his hand upon the miniature sword which hung at his side. All eyes were fixed upon the fatal stone, when from behind it was seen slowly to push forth, first a dirty wrinkled leg, then half a dirty wrinkled head, with one gleaming eye. It was too much; with cries of, "It is he! he comes! he spits! he pursues us!" the young guests of the château fled in good earnest, and never stopped until they reached the fountain and the fish-pond.

But Monsieur the Viscount stood his ground.

At the sudden apparition the blood rushed to his heart, and made him very white, then it flooded back again and made him very red, and then he fairly drew his sword, and shouting, " *Vive la France!*" rushed upon the enemy. The sword if small was sharp, and stabbed the poor toad would most undoubtedly have been, but for a sudden check received by the valiant little nobleman. It came in the shape of a large heavy hand that seized Monsieur the Viscount with the grasp of a giant, while a voice which could only have belonged to the owner of such a hand said in slow deep tones,

"*Que faites-vous?*" (" What are you doing?")

It was the tutor, who had been pacing up and down the terrace with a book, and who now stood holding the book in his right hand, and our hero in his left.

Monsieur the Viscount's tutor was a remarkable man. If he had not been so, he would hardly have been tolerated at the château, since he was not particularly beautiful, and not especially refined. He was in holy orders, as his tonsured head and clerical costume bore witness —a costume which, from its tightness and simplicity, only served to exaggerate the unusual proportions of his person. Monsieur the Pre-

ceptor had English blood in his veins, and his
northern origin betrayed itself in his towering
height and corresponding breadth, as well as by
his fair hair and light blue eyes. But the most
remarkable parts of his outward man were his
hands, which were of immense size, especially
about the thumbs. Monsieur the Preceptor
was not exactly in keeping with his present
abode. It was not only that he was wanting in
the grace and beauty that reigned around him,
but that his presence made those very graces
and beauties to look small. He seemed to have
a gift the reverse of that bestowed upon King
Midas—the gold on which his heavy hand was
laid seemed to become rubbish. In the presence
of the late Viscount, and in that of Madame his
widow, you would have felt fully the deep im-
portance of your dress being *à la mode,* and your
complexion *à la* strawberries and cream (such
influences still exist); but let the burly tutor
appear upon the scene, and all the magic died
at once out of brocaded silks and pearl-coloured
stockings, and dress and complexion became
subjects almost of insignificance. Monsieur
the Preceptor was certainly a singular man to
have been chosen as an inmate of such a household; but, though young, he had unusual talents,

and added to them the not more usual accompaniments of modesty and trustworthiness. To crown all, he was rigidly pious in times when piety was not fashionable, and an obedient son of the church of which he was a minister. Moreover, a family that fashion does not permit to be demonstratively religious, may gain a reflected credit from an austere chaplain ; and so Monsieur the Preceptor remained in the château and went his own way. It was this man who now laid hands on the Viscount, and, in a voice that sounded like amiable thunder, made the inquiry, " *Que faites-vous ?*"

" I am going to kill this animal—this hideous horrible animal," said Monsieur the Viscount, struggling vainly under the grasp of the tutor's finger and thumb.

" It is only a toad," said Monsieur the Preceptor, in his laconic tones.

" *Only* a toad, do you say, Monsieur ?" said the Viscount. " That is enough, I think. It will bite—it will spit—it will poison : it is like that dragon you tell me of, that devastated Rhodes—I am the good knight that shall kill it."

Monsieur the Preceptor laughed heartily. " You are misled by a vulgar error. Toads do not bite—they have no teeth; neither do they spit poison."

"You are wrong, Monsieur," said the Viscount; "I have seen their teeth myself. Claude Mignon, at the lodge, has two terrible ones, which he keeps in his pocket as a charm."

"I have seen them," said the tutor, "in Monsieur Claude's pocket. When he can show me similar ones in a toad's head I will believe. Meanwhile, I must beg of you, Monsieur, to put up your sword. You must not kill this poor animal, which is quite harmless, and very useful in a garden—it feeds upon many insects and reptiles which injure the plants."

"It shall not be useful in this garden," said the little Viscount, fretfully. "There are plenty of gardeners to destroy the insects, and if needful, we can have more. But the toad shall not remain. My mother would faint if she saw so hideous a beast among her beautiful flowers."

"Jacques!" roared the tutor to a gardener who was at some distance. Jacques started as if a clap of thunder had sounded in his ear, and approached with low bows. "Take that toad, Jacques, and carry it to the *potager*. It will keep the slugs from your cabbages."

Jacques bowed low and lower, and scratched

his head, and then did reverence again with Asiatic humility, but at the same time moved gradually backwards, and never even looked at the toad.

"You also have seen the contents of Monsieur Claude's pocket?" said the tutor, significantly, and quitting his hold of the Viscount, he stooped down, seized the toad in his huge finger and thumb, and strode off in the direction of the *potager*, followed at a respectful distance by Jacques, who vented his awe and astonishment in alternate bows and exclamations at the astounding conduct of the incomprehensible Preceptor.

"What is the use of such ugly beasts?" said the Viscount to his tutor, on his return from the *potager*. "Birds and butterflies are pretty, but what can such villains as these toads have been made for?"

"You should study natural history, Monsieur—" began the Priest, who was himself a naturalist.

"That is what you always say," interrupted the Viscount, with the perverse folly of ignorance; "but if I knew as much as you do, it would not make me understand why such ugly creatures need have been made."

"Nor," said the priest, firmly, "is it necessary that you should understand it, particularly
if you do not care to inquire. It is enough for
you and me if we remember Who made them,
some six thousand years before either of us
were born."

With which Monsieur the Preceptor (who
had all this time kept his place in the little book
with his big thumb) returned to the terrace, and
resumed his devotions at the point where they
had been interrupted; which exercise he continued till he was joined by the Curé of the village, and the two priests relaxed in the political
and religious gossip of the day.

Monsieur the Viscount rejoined his young
guests, and they fed the gold fish and the swans,
and played *Colin Maillard* in the shady walks,
and made a beautiful bouquet for Madame, and
then fled indoors at the first approach of evening
chill, and found that the Viscountess had prepared a feast of fruit and flowers for them in
the great hall. Here, at the head of the table,
with Madame at his right hand, his guests
around, and the liveried lacqueys waiting his
commands, Monsieur the Viscount forgot that
anything had ever been made which could mar
beauty and enjoyment; while the two priests

L

outside stalked up and down under the falling twilight, and talked ugly talk of crime and poverty that were *somewhere* now, and of troubles to come hereafter.

And so night fell over the beautiful sky, the beautiful château, and the beautiful gardens; and upon the secure slumbers of beautiful Madame and her beautiful son, and beautiful, beautiful France.

CHAPTER II.

It was the year of grace 1792, thirteen years after the events related in the last chapter. It was the 2nd of September, and Sunday, a day of rest and peace in all Christian countries, and even more in gay, beautiful France—a day of festivity and merriment. This Sunday, however, seemed rather an exception to the general rule. There were no gay groups or bannered processions; the typical incense and the public devotion of which it is the symbol were alike wanting; the streets in some places seemed deserted, and in others there was an ominous crowd, and the dreary silence was now and then broken by a distant sound of yells and cries, that struck terror into the hearts of the Parisians.

It was a deserted bye-street overlooked by some shut-up warehouses, and from the cellar of one of these a young man crept up on to the pathway. His dress had once been beautiful, but it was torn and soiled; his face was beautiful still, but it was marred by the hideous eagerness of a face on which famine has laid her hand—he was starving. As this man came out from the warehouse, another man came down the street. His dress was not beautiful, neither was he. There was a red look about him—he wore a red flannel cap, tricolor ribbons, and had something red upon his hands, which was neither ribbon nor flannel. He also looked hungry; but it was not for food. The other stopped when he saw him, and pulled something from his pocket. It was a watch, a repeater, in a gold filigree case of exquisite workmanship, with raised figures depicting the loves of an Arcadian shepherd and shepherdess; and, as it lay on the white hand of its owner, it bore an evanescent fragrance that seemed to recall scenes as beautiful and as completely past as the days of pastoral perfection, when—

> "All the world and love were young,
> And truth in every shepherd's tongue."

The young man held it to the other and spoke. " It was my mother's," he said, with an appealing glance of violet eyes ; " I would not part with it, but that I am starving. Will you get me food?"

"You are hiding?" said he of the red cap.

" Is that a crime in these days?" said the other, with a smile that would in other days have been irresistible.

The man took the watch, shaded the donor's beautiful face with a rough red cap and tricolor ribbon, and bade him follow him. He, who had but lately come to Paris, dragged his exhausted body after his conductor, hardly noticed the crowds in the streets, the signs by which the man got free passage for them both, or their entrance by a little side-door into a large dark building, and never knew till he was delivered to one of the gaolers that he had been led into the prison of the Abbaye. Then the wretch tore the cap of liberty from his victim's head, and pointed to him with a fierce laugh.

" He wants food, this aristocrat. He shall not wait long—there is a feast in the court be-low, which he shall join presently. See to it, Antoine ! and you *Monsieur, Mons-ieur !* listen to the banqueters."

He ceased, and in the silence yells and cries

from a court below came up like some horrid answer to imprecation.

The man continued—

"He has paid for his admission, this Monsieur. It belonged to Madame his mother. Behold!"

He held the watch above his head, and dashed it with insane fury on the ground, and bidding the gaoler see to his prisoner, rushed away to the court below.

The prisoner needed some attention. Weakness and fasting and horror had overpowered a delicate body and a sensitive mind, and he lay senseless by the shattered relic of happier times. Antoine the gaoler (a weak-minded man, whom circumstances had made cruel), looked at him with indifference while the Jacobin remained in the place, and with half-suppressed pity when he had gone. The place where he lay was a hall or passage in the prison, into which several cells opened, and a number of the prisoners were gathered together at one end of it. One of them had watched the proceedings of the Jacobin and his victim with profound interest, and now advanced to where the poor youth lay. He was a priest, and though thirteen years had passed over his head since we saw him in the château, and though toil and suffering and anxiety had added the traces of as many more : yet it would not have been difficult to recognize the towering height, the candid face, and finally the large thumb in the little book of ——, Monsieur the Preceptor, who had years ago exchanged his old position for a parochial cure. He strode up to the gaoler (whose head came a little above the priest's elbow), and drawing him aside, asked with his old abruptness, " Who is this ?"

" It is the Vicomte de B——. I know his face. He has escaped the commissaires for some days."

" I thought so. Is his name on the registers ?"

" No. He escaped arrest, and has just been brought in as you saw."

" Antoine," said the Priest, in a low voice, and with a gaze that seemed to pierce the soul of the weak little gaoler; " Antoine, when you were a shoemaker in the Rue de la Croix, in two or three hard winters I think you found me a friend."

" Oh! Monsieur le Curé," said Antoine, writhing; " if Monsieur le Curé would believe that if I could save his life! but—"

" Pshaw ! " said the Priest, " it is not for

myself, but for this boy. You must save him, Antoine. Hear me, you *must*. Take him now to one of the lower cells and hide him. You risk nothing. His name is not on the prison register. He will not be called, he will not be missed; that fanatic will think that he has perished with the rest of us;" (Antoine shuddered, though the priest did not move a muscle;) "and when this mad fever has subsided and order is restored, he will reward you. And Antoine—"

Here the Priest pocketed his book and somewhat awkwardly with his huge hands unfastened the left side of his cassock, and tore the silk from the lining. Monsieur the Curé's cassock seemed a cabinet of oddities. First he pulled from this ingenious hiding-place a crucifix, which he replaced; then a knot of white ribbon which he also restored; and finally a tiny pocket or bag of what had been cream-coloured satin embroidered with small bunches of heartsease, and which was aromatic with otto of roses. Awkwardly, and somewhat slowly he drew out of this a small locket, in the centre of which was some unreadable legend in cabalistic-looking character, and which blazed with the finest diamonds. Heaven alone knows the secret of that gem, or the struggle with which the Priest yielded it. He put it into Antoine's hand, talking as he did so, partly to himself and partly to the gaoler.

"We brought nothing into this world, and it is certain we can carry nothing out. The diamonds are of the finest, Antoine, and will sell for much. The blessing of a dying priest upon you if you do kindly, and his curse if you do ill to this poor child, whose home was my home in better days. And for the locket,—it is but a remembrance, and to remember is not difficult !"

As the last observation was not addressed to Antoine, so also he did not hear it. He was discontentedly watching the body of the Viscount, whom he consented to help, but with genuine weak-mindedness consented ungraciously.

"How am I to get him there? Monsieur le Curé sees that he cannot stand upon his feet ! "

Monsieur le Curé smiled, and stooping, picked his old pupil up in his arms as if he had been a baby, and bore him to one of the doors.

"You must come no further," said Antoine hastily.

"Ingrate ! " muttered the Priest in momentary anger, and then ashamed, he crossed himself and pressing the young nobleman to his bosom with the last gush of earthly affection that he was to feel, he kissed his senseless face, spoke a benediction to ears that could not hear it, and laid his burden down.

"God the Father, the Son, and the Holy Ghost, be with thee now and in the dread hour of death. Adieu! we shall meet hereafter."

The look of pity, the yearning of rekindled love, the struggle of silenced memories passed from his face and left a shining calm—foretaste of the perpetual Light and the eternal Rest.

Before he reached the other prisoners, the large thumb had found its old place in the little book, the lips formed the old old words; but it might almost have been said of him already, that " his spirit was with the God who gave it."

As for Monsieur the Viscount, it was perhaps well that he was not too sensible of his position, for Antoine got him down the flight of stone steps that led to the cell by the simple process of dragging him by the heels. After a similar fashion he crossed the floor, and was deposited on a pallet; the gaoler then emptied a broken pitcher of water over his face, and locking the door securely, hurried back to his charge.

When Monsieur the Viscount came to his senses he raised himself and looked round his new abode. It was a small stone cell; it was underground, with a little grated window at the top that seemed to be level with the court; there was a pallet—painfully pressed and worn, —a chair, a stone on which stood a plate and broken pitcher, and in one corner a huge bundle of firewood which mocked a place where there was no fire. Stones lay scattered about, the walls were black, and in the far dark corners the wet oozed out and trickled slowly down, and lizards and other reptiles crawled up.

I suppose that the first object that attracts the hopes of a new prisoner is the window of his cell, and to this, despite his weakness, Monsieur the Viscount crept. It afforded him little satisfaction. It was too high in the cell for him to reach it, too low in the prison to command any view, and was securely grated with iron. Then he examined the walls, but not a stone was loose. As he did so, his eye fell upon the floor, and he noticed that two of the stones that lay about had been raised up by some one and a third laid upon the top. It looked like child's play, and Monsieur the Viscount kicked it down, and then he saw that underneath it there was a pellet of paper roughly rolled together. Evidently it was something left by the former oc-

cupant of the cell for his successor. Perhaps he
had begun some plan for getting away which he
had not had time to perfect on his own account.
Perhaps—but by this time the paper was spread
out, and Monsieur the Viscount read the writing.
The paper was old and yellow. It was the fly-
leaf torn out of a little book, and on it was
written in black chalk, the words—

" Souvenez-vous du Sauveur."

(Remember the Saviour.)

He turned it over, he turned it back again;
there was no other mark; there was nothing
more; and Monsieur the Viscount did not con-
ceal from himself that he was disappointed.
How could it be otherwise? He had been bred
in ease and luxury, and surrounded with everything that could make life beautiful; while
ugliness, and want, and sickness, and all that
make life miserable, had been kept, as far as
they can be kept, from the precincts of the
beautiful château which was his home. What
were the *consolations* of religion to him? They
are offered to those (and to those only) who
need them. They were to Monsieur the Viscount, what the Crucified Christ was to the
Greeks of old—foolishness.

He put the paper in his pocket and lay down again, feeling it the crowning disappointment of what he had lately suffered. Presently, Antoine came with some food; it was not dainty, but Monsieur the Viscount devoured it like a famished hound, and then made inquiries as to how he came and how long he had been there. When the gaoler began to describe him, whom he called the Curé, Monsieur the Viscount's attention quickened into eagerness, an eagerness deepened by the tender interest that always hangs round the names of those whom we have known in happier and younger days. The happy memories recalled by hearing of his old tutor seemed to blot out his present misfortunes. With French excitability, he laughed and wept alternately.

"As burly as ever, you say? The little book? I remember it, it was his breviary. Ah! it is he. It is Monsieur the Preceptor, whom I have not seen for years. Take me to him, bring him here, let me see him!"

But Monsieur the Preceptor was in Paradise.

That first night of Monsieur the Viscount's imprisonment was a terrible one. The bitter chill of a Parisian autumn, the gnawings of half-satisfied hunger, the thick walls that shut out all hope of escape but did not exclude those fearful cries that lasted with few intervals throughout the night, made it like some hideous dream. At last the morning broke; at half-past two o'clock, some members of the *commune* presented themselves in the hall of the National Assembly with the significant anouncement:—" The prisons are empty !" and Antoine, who had been quaking for hours, took courage, and went with half a loaf of bread and a pitcher of water to the cell that was not " empty." He found his prisoner struggling with a knot of white ribbon, which he was trying to fasten in his hair. One glance at his face told all.

" It is the fever," said Antoine; and he put down the bread and water and fetched an old blanket and a pillow; and that day and for many days, the gaoler hung above his prisoner's pallet with the tenderness of a woman. Was he haunted by the vision of a burly figure that had bent over his own sick bed in the Rue, de la Croix? Did the voice (once so familiar in counsel and benediction !) echo still in his ears?

" *The blessing of a dying priest upon you if you do well, and his curse if you do ill to this poor child, whose home was my home in better days.*"

Be this as it may, Antoine tended his patient with all the constancy compatible with keeping his presence in the prison a secret; and it was not till the crisis was safely past, that he began to visit the cell less frequently, and reassumed the harsh manners which he held to befit his office.

Monsieur the Viscount's mind rambled much in his illness. He called for his mother, who had long been dead. He fancied himself in his own château. He thought that all his servants stood in a body before him, but that not one would move to wait on him. He thought that he had abundance of the most tempting food and cooling drinks, but placed just beyond his reach. He thought that he saw two lights like stars near together, which were close to the ground, and kept appearing and then vanishing away. In time he became more sensible; the château melted into the stern reality of his prison walls; the delicate food became bread and water; the servants disappeared like spectres; but in the empty cell, in the dark corners near the floor, he still fancied that he saw two sparks of light coming and going, appearing and then vanishing away. He watched them till his giddy head would bear it no longer, and he closed his eyes and slept. When he awoke he was much better, but when he raised himself and turned towards the stone—there, by the bread and the broken pitcher, sat a dirty, ugly, wrinkled toad, gazing at him, Monsieur the Viscount, with eyes of yellow fire.

Monsieur the Viscount had long ago forgotten the toad which had alarmed his childhood; but his national dislike to that animal had not been lessened by years, and the toad of the prison seemed likely to fare no better than the toad of the château. He dragged himself from his pallet, and took up one of the large damp stones which lay about the floor of the cell, to throw at the intruder. He expected that when he approached it, the toad would crawl away, and that he could throw the stone after it: but to his surprise, the beast sat quite unmoved, looking at him with calm shining eyes, and somehow or other, Monsieur the Viscount lacked strength or heart to kill it. He stood doubtful for a moment, and then a sudden feeling of weakness obliged him to drop the stone, and sit down, while tears sprang to his eyes with the sense of his helplessness.

"Why should I kill it?" he said bitterly. "The beast will live and grow fat upon this damp and loathsomeness, long after they have put an end to my feeble life. It shall remain. The cell is not big, but it is big enough for us both. However large be the rooms a man builds himself to live in, it needs but little space in which to die!"

So Monsieur the Viscount dragged his pallet away from the toad, placed another stone by it, and removed the pitcher; and then, wearied with his efforts, lay down and slept heavily.

When he awoke, on the new stone by the pitcher was the toad, staring full at him with topaz eyes. He lay still this time and did not move, for the animal showed no intention of spitting, and he was puzzled by its tameness.

"It seems to like the sight of a man," he thought. "Is it possible that any former inmate of this wretched prison can have amused his solitude by making a pet of such a creature? and if there were such a man, where is he now?"

Henceforward, sleeping or waking, whenever Monsieur the Viscount lay down upon his pallet, the toad crawled up on to the stone, and kept watch over him with shining lustrous eyes; but whenever there was a sound of the key grating in the lock, and the gaoler coming his rounds, away crept the toad, and was quickly lost in the dark corners of the room. When the man was gone, it returned to its place, and Monsieur the Viscount would talk to it, as he lay on his pallet.

"Ah! Monsieur Crapaud," he would say with mournful pleasantry, "without doubt you have had a master and a kind one; but tell me who was he, and where is he now? Was he old or young, and was it in the last stage of maddening loneliness that he made friends with such a creature as you?"

Monsieur Crapaud looked very intelligent, but he made no reply, and Monsieur the Viscount had recourse to Antoine.

"Who was in this cell before me?" he asked at the gaoler's next visit.

Antoine's face clouded. "Monsieur le Curé had this room. My orders were that he was to be imprisoned 'in secret.'"

Monsieur le Curé had this room. There was a revelation in those words. It was all explained now. The Priest had always had a love for animals (and for ugly, common animals), which his pupil had by no means shared. His room at the château had been little less than a menagerie. He had even kept a glass beehive there, which communicated with a hole in the window through which the bees flew in and out, and

M

he would stand for hours with his thumb in the breviary, watching the labours of his pets. And this also had been his room! This dark, damp cell. Here, breviary in hand, he had stood, and lain, and knelt. Here, in this miserable prison, he had found something to love, and on which to expend the rare intelligence and benevolence of his nature. Here, finally, in the last hours of his life, he had written on the fly-leaf of his prayer-book something to comfort his successor, and "being dead yet spoke" the words of consolation which he had administered in his lifetime. Monsieur the Viscount read that paper now with different feelings.

There is perhaps no argument so strong, and no virtue that so commands the respect of young men, as consistency. Monsieur the Preceptor's lifelong counsel and example would have done less for his pupil than was effected by the knowledge of his consistent career, now that it was past. It was not the nobility of the Priest's principles that awoke in Monsieur the Viscount a desire to imitate his religious example, but the fact that he had applied them to his own life, not only in the time of wealth, but in the time of tribulation and in the hour of death. All that high-strung piety—that life of prayer

—those unswerving admonitions to consider the vanity of earthly treasures, and to prepare for death—which had sounded so unreal amidst the perfumed elegancies of the château, came back now with a reality gained from experiment. The daily life of self-denial, the conversation garnished from Scripture and from the Fathers, had not, after all, been mere priestly affectations. In no symbolic manner, but literally, he had "watched for the coming of his Lord," and "taken up the cross daily;" and so, when the cross was laid on him, and when the voice spoke which must speak to all, "The Master is come, and calleth for thee," he bore the burden and obeyed the summons unmoved.

Unmoved!—this was the fact that struck deep into the heart of Monsieur the Viscount, as he listened to Antoine's account of the Curé's imprisonment. What had astonished and overpowered his own undisciplined nature had not disturbed Monsieur the Preceptor. He had prayed in the château—he prayed in the prison. He had often spoken in the château of the softening and comforting influences of communion with the lower animals and with nature, and in the uncertainty of imprisonment he had tamed a toad. "None of these things had moved him," and, in a storm of grief and admiration, Monsieur the Viscount bewailed the memory of his tutor.

"If he had only lived to teach me!"

But he was dead, and there was nothing for Monsieur the Viscount but to make the most of his example. This was not so easy to follow as he imagined. Things seemed to be different with him to what they had been with Monsieur the Preceptor. He had no lofty meditations, no ardent prayers, and calm and peace seemed more distant than ever. Monsieur the Viscount met, in short, with all those difficulties that the soul must meet with, which, in a moment of enthusiasm, has resolved upon a higher and a better way of life, and in moments of depression is perpetually tempted to forego that resolution. His prison life was, however, a pretty severe discipline, and he held on with struggles and prayers; and so, little by little, and day by day, as the time of his imprisonment went by, the consolations of religion became a daily strength against the fretfulness of imperious temper, the sickness of hope deferred, and the dark suggestions of despair.

The term of his imprisonment was a long one. Many prisoners came and went within the walls of the Abbaye, but Monsieur the Viscount still remained in his cell: indeed, he would have gained little by leaving it if he could have done so, as he would almost certainly have been retaken. As it was, Antoine on more than one occasion concealed him behind the bundles of firewood, and once or twice he narrowly escaped detection by less friendly officials. There were times when the guillotine seemed to him almost better than this long suspense: but while other heads passed to the block, his remained on his shoulders; and so weeks and even months went by. And during all this time, sleeping or waking, whenever he lay down upon his pallet, the toad crept up on to the stone, and kept watch over him with lustrous eyes.

Monsieur the Viscount hardly acknowledged to himself the affection with which he came to regard this ugly and despicable animal. The greater part of his regard for it he believed to be due to its connection with his tutor, and the rest he set down to the score of his own humanity, and took credit to himself accordingly: whereas in truth Monsieur Crapaud was of incalculable service to his new master, who would lie and chatter to him for hours, and almost forget his present discomfort in recalling past happiness, as he described the château, the gardens, the burly tutor, and beautiful Madame, or laughed over his childish remembrances of the toad's teeth in Claude Mignon's pocket; whilst Monsieur Crapaud sat well-bred and silent, with a world of comprehension in his fiery eyes. Whoever thinks this puerile must remember that my hero was a Frenchman, and a young Frenchman, with a prescriptive right to chatter for chattering's sake, and also that he had not a very highly cultivated mind of his own to converse with, even if the most highly cultivated intellect is ever a reliable resource against the terrors of solitary confinement.

Foolish or wise, however, Monsieur the Viscount's attachment strengthened daily; and one day something happened which showed his pet in a new light, and afforded him fresh amusement.

The prison was much infested with certain large black spiders, which crawled about the floor and walls; and, as Monsieur the Viscount was lying on his pallet, he saw one of these scramble up and over the stone on which sat Monsieur Crapaud. That good gentleman, whose eyes, till then, had been fixed as usual

on his master, now turned his attention to the
intruder. The spider, as if conscious of danger,
had suddenly stopped still. Monsieur Crapaud
gazed at it intently with his beautiful eyes, and
bent himself slightly forward. So they remained
for some seconds, then the spider turned round,
and began suddenly to scramble away. At this
instant Monsieur the Viscount saw his friend's
eyes gleam with an intenser fire, his head was
jerked forwards; it almost seemed as if something had been projected from his mouth, and
drawn back again with the rapidity of lightning.
Then Monsieur Crapaud resumed his position,
drew in his head, and gazed mildly and sedately
before him; *but the spider was nowhere to be
seen.*

Monsieur the Viscount burst into a loud
laugh.

"Eh, well! Monsieur," said he, "but this is
not well-bred on your part. Who gave you
leave to eat my spiders? and to bolt them in
such an unmannerly way, moreover."

In spite of this reproof Monsieur Crapaud
looked in no way ashamed of himself, and I regret to state that henceforward (with the partial
humaneness of mankind in general), Monsieur
the Viscount amused himself by catching the

insects (which were only too plentiful) in an old oyster-shell, and setting them at liberty on the stone for the benefit of his friend. As for him, all appeared to be fish that came to his net— spiders and beetles, slugs and snails from the damp corners, flies, and wood-lice found on turning up the large stone, disappeared one after the other. The wood-lice were an especial amusement: when Monsieur the Viscount touched them, they shut up into tight little balls, and in this condition he removed them to the stone, and placed them like marbles in a row, Monsieur Crapaud watching the proceeding with rapt attention. After awhile the balls would slowly open and begin to crawl away; but he was a very active wood-louse indeed who escaped the suction of Monsieur Crapaud's tongue, as, his eyes glowing with eager enjoyment, he bolted one after the other, and Monsieur the Viscount clapped his hands and applauded.

The grated window was a very fine field for spiders and other insects, and by piling up stones on the floor, Monsieur the Viscount contrived to scramble up to it, and fill his friend's oyster-shell with the prey.

One day, about a year and nine months since his first arrival at the prison, he climbed to the embrasure of the window, as usual, oyster-shell in hand. He always chose a time for this when he knew that the court would most probably be deserted, to avoid the danger of being recognized through the grating. He was, therefore, not a little startled by being disturbed in his capture of a fat black spider by a sound of something bumping against the iron bars. On looking up, he saw that a string was dangling before the window with something attached to the end of it. He drew it in, and, as he did so, he fancied that he heard a distant sound of voices and clapped hands, as if from some window above. He proceeded to examine his prize, and found that it was a little round pincushion of sand, such as women use to polish their needles with, and that, apparently, it was used as a make-weight to ensure the steady descent of a neat little letter that was tied beside it, in company with a small lead pencil. The letter was directed to *" The prisoner who finds this."* Monsieur the Viscount opened it at once. This was the letter :—

" In prison, 24th Prairial, year 2.

" Fellow-sufferer, who are you? how long have you been imprisoned? Be good enough to answer."

Monsieur the Viscount hesitated for a moment, and then determined to risk all. He tore off a bit of the paper, and with the little pencil hurriedly wrote this reply :—

"*In secret, June* 12, 1794.

"*Louis Archambaud Jean-Marie Arnaud, Vicomte de B., supposed to have perished in the massacres of September,* 1792. *Keep my secret. I have been imprisoned a year and nine months. Who are* you? *how long have* you *been here ?*"

The letter was drawn up, and he watched anxiously for the reply. It came, and with it some sheets of blank paper.

"*Monsieur,—We have the honour to reply to your inquiries, and thank you for your frankness. Henri Edouard Clermont, Baron de St. Claire. Valerie de St. Claire. We have been here but two days. Accept our sympathy for your misfortunes.*"

Four words in this note seized at once upon Monsieur the Viscount's interest—*Valerie de St. Claire ;*—and for some reasons which I do not pretend to explain, he decided that it was she who was the author of these epistles, and the demon of curiosity forthwith took possession of his mind. Who was she? was she old or young? And in which relation did she stand to Monsieur le Baron—that of wife, of sister, or of daughter? And from some equally inexplicable cause Monsieur the Viscount determined in his own mind that it was the latter. To make assurance doubly sure, however, he laid a trap to discover the real state of the case. He wrote a letter of thanks and sympathy, expressed with all the delicate chivalrous politeness of a nobleman of the old *régime*, and addressed it to *Madame la Baronne*. The plan succeeded. The next note he received contained these sentences : —" *I am not the Baroness. Madame my mother is, alas! dead. I and my father are alone. He is ill; but thanks you, Monsieur, for your letters, which relieve the* ennui *of imprisonment. Are you alone?*"

Monsieur the Viscount, as in duty bound, relieved the *ennui* of the Baron's captivity by another epistle. Before answering the last question, he turned round involuntarily, and looked to where Monsieur Crapaud sat by the broken pitcher. The beautiful eyes were turned towards him, and Monsieur the Viscount took up his pencil, and wrote hastily, "*I am not alone—I have a friend.*"

Henceforward the oyster-shell took a long time to fill, and patience seemed a harder virtue than ever. Perhaps the last fact had something to do with the rapid decline of Monsieur the Viscount's health. He became paler and weaker, and more fretful. His prayers were accompanied by greater mental struggles, and watered with more tears. He was, however, most positive in his assurances to Monsieur Crapaud that he knew the exact nature and cause of the malady that was consuming him. It resulted, he said, from the noxious and unwholesome condition of his cell; and he would entreat Antoine to have it swept out. After some difficulty the gaoler consented.

It was nearly a month since Monsieur the Viscount had first been startled by the appearance of the little pincushion. The stock of paper had long been exhausted. He had torn up his cambric ruffles to write upon, and Mademoiselle de St. Claire had made havoc of her pocket-handkerchiefs for the same purpose. The Viscount was feebler than ever, and Antoine became alarmed. The cell should be swept out the next morning. He would come himself, he said, and bring another man out of the town with him to help him, for the work was heavy,

and he had a touch of rheumatism. The man
was a stupid fellow from the country, who had
only been a week in Paris; he had never heard
of the Viscount, and Antoine would tell him
that the prisoner was a certain young lawyer
who had really died of fever in prison the day
before. Monsieur the Viscount thanked him;
and it was not till the next morning arrived,
and he was expecting them every moment, that
Monsieur the Viscount remembered the toad,
and that he would without doubt be swept away
with the rest in the general clearance. At first
he thought that he would beg them to leave it,
but some knowledge of the petty insults which
that class of men heaped upon their prisoners
made him feel that this would probably be only
an additional reason for their taking the animal away. There was no place to hide it in,
for they would go all round the room; unless—
unless Monsieur the Viscount took it up in his
hand. And this was just what he objected to
do. All his old feelings of repugnance came
back; he had not even got gloves on; his long
white hands were bare, he could not touch a
toad. It was true that the beast had amused
him, and that he had chatted to it; but after
all, this was a piece of childish folly—an un-

manly way, to say the least, of relieving the tedium of captivity. What was Monsieur Crapaud but a very ugly (and most people said a venomous) reptile? To what a folly he had been condescending! With these thoughts, Monsieur the Viscount steeled himself against the glances of his topaz-eyed friend, and when the steps of the men were heard upon the stairs, he did not move from the window where he had placed himself, with his back to the stone.

The steps came nearer and nearer, Monsieur the Viscount began to whistle;—the key was rattled into the lock, and Monsieur the Viscount heard a bit of bread fall, as the toad hastily descended to hide itself as usual in the corners. In a moment his resolution was gone; another second, and it would be too late. He dashed after the creature, picked it up, and when the men came in he was standing with his hands behind him, in which Monsieur Crapaud was quietly and safely seated.

The room was swept, and Antoine was preparing to go, when the other, who had been eyeing the prisoner suspiciously, stopped and said with a sharp sneer, "Does the citizen always preserve that position?"

"Not he," said the gaoler, good-naturedly. "He spends most of his time in bed, which saves his legs. Come along, François."

"I shall not come," said the other, obstinately. "Let the citizen show me his hands."

"Plague take you!" said Antoine, in a whisper. "What sulky fit possesses you, my comrade? Let the poor wretch alone. What wouldst thou with his hands? Wait a little, and thou shalt have his head."

"We should have few heads or prisoners either, if thou hadst the care of them," said François sharply. "I say that the prisoner secretes something, and that I will see it. Show your hands, dog of an aristocrat!"

Monsieur the Viscount set his teeth to keep himself from speaking, and held out his hands in silence, toad and all.

Both the men started back with an exclamation, and François got behind his comrade, and swore over his shoulder.

Monsieur the Viscount stood upright and still, with a smile on his white face. "Behold, citizen, what I secrete, and what I desire to keep. Behold all that I have left to secrete or to desire! There is nothing more."

"Throw it down!" screamed François; "many

a witch has been burnt for less — throw it
down."

The colour began to flood over Monsieur the
Viscount's face; but still he spoke gently, and
with bated breath. "If you wish me to suffer,
citizen, let this be my witness that I have suffered. I must be very friendless to desire such
a friend. I must be brought very low to ask
such a favour. Let the Republic give me this."

"The Republic has one safe rule for aristocrats," said the other; "she gives them nothing
but their keep till she pays for their shaving—
once for all. She gave one of these dogs a few
rags to dress a wound on his back with, and he
made a rope of his dressings, and let himself
down from the window. We will have no more
such games. You may be training the beast to
spit poison at good citizens. Throw it down
and kill it."

Monsieur the Viscount made no reply. His
hands had moved towards his breast, against
which he was holding his golden-eyed friend.
There are times in life when the brute creation
contrasts favourably with the lords thereof, and
this was one of them. It was hard to part just
now.

Antoine, who had been internally cursing his

own folly in bringing such a companion into the cell, now interfered. "If you are going to stay here to be bitten or spit at, François, my friend," said he, "I am not. Thou art zealous, my comrade, but dull as an owl. The Republic is far-sighted in her wisdom beyond thy coarse ideas, and has more ways of taking their heads from these aristocrats than one. Dost thou not see?" And he tapped his forehead significantly, and looked at the prisoner; and so, between talking and pushing, got his sulky companion out of the cell, and locked the door after them.

"And so, my friend—my friend!" said Monsieur the Viscount, tenderly, "we are safe once more; but it will not be for long, my Crapaud. Something tells me that I cannot much longer be overlooked. A little while, and I shall be gone; and thou wilt have, perchance, another master, when I am summoned before mine."

Monsieur the Viscount's misgivings were just. François, on whose stupidity Antoine had relied, was (as is not uncommon with people stupid in other respects) just clever enough to be mischievous. Antoine's evident alarm made him suspicious, and he began to talk about the too-

N

elegant-looking young lawyer who was imprisoned " in secret," and permitted by the gaoler to
keep venomous beasts.   Antoine was examined
and committed to one of his own cells, and
Monsieur the Viscount was summoned before
the revolutionary tribunal.

There was little need even for the scanty
inquiry that in those days preceded sentence.
In every line of his beautiful face, marred as
it was by sickness and suffering—in the un-
conquerable dignity, which dirt and raggedness
were powerless to hide, the fatal nobility of his
birth and breeding were betrayed.   When he
returned to the ante-room, he did not positively
know his fate; but in his mind there was a
moral certainty that left him no hope.

The room was filled with other prisoners await-
ing trial; and, as he entered, his eyes wandered
round it to see if there were any familiar faces.
They fell upon two figures standing with their
backs to him—a tall, fierce-looking man, who,
despite his height and fierceness, had a restless,
nervous despondency expressed in all his move-
ments; and a young girl who leant on his arm
as if for support, but whose steady quietude gave
her more the air of a supporter.   Without seeing their faces, and for no reasonable reason,

Monsieur the Viscount decided with himself that
they were the Baron and his daughter, and he
begged the man who was conducting him for a
moment's delay. The man consented. France
was becoming sick of unmitigated carnage, and
even the executioners sometimes indulged in
pity by way of a change.

As Monsieur the Viscount approached the
two they turned round, and he saw her face—
a very fair and very resolute one, with ashen
hair and large eyes. In common with almost
all the faces in that room, it was blanched with
suffering; and, it is fair to say, in common with
many of them, it was pervaded by a lofty calm.
Monsieur the Viscount never for an instant
doubted his own conviction; he drew near and
said in a low voice, " Mademoiselle de St.
Claire !"

The Baron looked first fierce, and then alarmed.
His daughter's face illumined; she turned her
large eyes on the speaker, and said simply,

" Monsieur le Vicomte ?"

The Baron apologized, commiserated, and sat
down on a seat near, with a look of fretful despair; and his daughter and Monsieur the Viscount were left standing together. Monsieur
the Viscount desired to say a great deal, and

could say very little. The moments went by, and hardly a word had been spoken.

Valerie asked if he knew his fate.

" I have not heard it," he said; " but I am morally certain. There can be but one end in these days."

She sighed. " It is the same with us. And if you must suffer, Monsieur, I wish that we may suffer together. It would comfort my father—and me."

Her composure vexed him. Just, too, when he was sensible that the desire of life was making a few fierce struggles in his own breast.

" You seem to look forward to death with great cheerfulness, Mademoiselle."

The large eyes were raised to him with a look of surprise at the irritation of his tone.

" I think," she said gently, " that one does not look forward *to*, but *beyond* it." She stopped and hesitated, still watching his face, and then spoke hurriedly and diffidently :—

" Monsieur, it seems impertinent to make such suggestions to you, who have doubtless a full fund of consolation; but I remember, when a child, going to hear the preaching of a monk who was famous for his eloquence. He said that his text was from the Scriptures—it has been in my mind all to-day—' *There the wicked cease from troubling, and there the weary are at rest.*' The man is becoming impatient. Adieu! Monsieur. A thousand thanks and a thousand blessings."

She offered her cheek, on which there was not a ray of increased colour, and Monsieur the Viscount stooped and kissed it, with a thick mist gathering in his eyes, through which he could not see her face.

"Adieu! Valerie!"

"Adieu! Louis!"

So they met, and so they parted; and as Monsieur the Viscount went back to his prison, he flattered himself that the last link was broken for him in the chain of earthly interests.

When he reached the cell he was tired, and lay down, and in a few seconds a soft scrambling over the floor announced the return of Monsieur Crapaud from his hiding-place. With one wrinkled leg after another he clambered on to the stone, and Monsieur the Viscount started when he saw him.

"Friend Crapaud! I had actually forgotten thee. I fancied I had said adieu for the last time;" and he gave a choked sigh, which Monsieur Crapaud could not be expected to understand. In about five minutes he sprang up suddenly. "Monsieur Crapaud, I have not long to live, and no time must be lost in making my will." Monsieur Crapaud was too wise to express any astonishment; and his master began to hunt for a tidy-looking stone (paper and cambric were both at an end). They were all rough and dirty; but necessity had made the Viscount inventive, and he took a couple and rubbed them together till he had polished both. Then he pulled out the little pencil, and for the next half hour composed and wrote busily. When it was done he lay down, and read it to his friend. This was Monsieur the Viscount's last will and testament:—

" To my successor in this cell.

" To you whom Providence has chosen to be " the inheritor of my sorrows and my captivity, " I desire to make another bequest. There is in " this prison a toad. He was tamed by a man " (peace to his memory!) who tenanted this cell " before me. He has been my friend and com- " panion for nearly two years of sad imprison- " ment. He has sat by my bedside, fed from " my hand, and shared all my confidence. He " is ugly, but he has beautiful eyes; he is silent,

"but he is attentive; he is a brute, but I wish
"the men of France were in this respect more
"his superiors! He is very faithful. May you
"never have a worse friend! He feeds upon
"insects, which I have been accustomed to pro-
"cure for him. Be kind to him; he will repay
"it. Like other men, I bequeath what I would
"take with me if I could.

"Fellow-sufferer, adieu! GOD comfort you
"as He has comforted me! The sorrows of this
"life are sharp but short; the joys of the next
"life are eternal. Think sometimes on him who
"commends his friend to your pity, and himself
"to your prayers.

"This is the last will and testament, of
"Louis Archambaud Jean-Marie Arnaud, Vi-
"comte de B——.''

Monsieur the Viscount's last will and testament was with difficulty squeezed into the sur-
face of the larger of the stones. Then he hid
it where the Priest had hid *his* bequest long ago,
and then lay down to dream of Monsieur the
Preceptor, and that they had met at last.

The next day was one of anxious suspense.
In the evening, as usual, a list of those who
were to be guillotined next morning, was brought
into the prison; and Monsieur the Viscount

begged for a sight of it. It was brought to him.
First on the list was Antoine! Halfway down
was his own name, " Louis de B—," and a little
lower his fascinated gaze fell upon names that
stirred his heart with such a passion of regret as
he had fancied it would never feel again, " Henri
de St. Claire, Valerie de St. Claire."

Her eyes seemed to shine on him from the
gathering twilight, and her calm voice to echo
in his ears. "*It has been in my mind all to-day.
There the wicked cease from troubling, and there
the weary are at rest.*"

There! He buried his face and prayed.

He was disturbed by the unlocking of the
door, and the new gaoler appeared with Antoine!
The poor wretch seemed overpowered by terror.
He had begged to be imprisoned for this last
night with Monsieur the Viscount. It was only
a matter of a few hours, as they were to die at
daybreak, and his request was granted.

Antoine's entrance turned the current of Monsieur the Viscount's thoughts. No more selfish
reflections now. He must comfort this poor
creature, of whose death he was to be the unin-
tentional cause. Antoine's first anxiety was that
Monsieur the Viscount should bear witness that
the gaoler had treated him kindly, and so earned

the blessing and not the curse of Monsieur le
Curé, whose powerful presence seemed to haunt
him still. On this score he was soon set at rest,
and then came the old, old story. He had been
but a bad man. If his life were to come over
again, he would do differently. Did Monsieur
the Viscount think that there was any hope?

Would Monsieur the Viscount have recognized
himself, could he, two years ago, have seen himself as he was now? Kneeling by that rough,
uncultivated figure, and pleading with all the
eloquence that he could master to that rough
uncultivated heart, the great Truths of Christianity,—so great and few and simple in their
application to our needs! The violet eyes had
never appealed more tenderly, the soft voice had
never been softer than now, as he strove to explain to this ignorant soul, the cardinal doctrines
of Faith and Repentance, and Charity, with an
earnestness that was perhaps more effectual than
his preaching.

Monsieur the Viscount was quite as much
astonished as flattered by the success of his instructions. The faith on which he had laid
hold with such mortal struggles, seemed almost
to "come natural" (as people say) to Antoine.
With abundant tears, he professed the deepest

penitence for his past life, at the same time that he accepted the doctrine of the Atonement as a natural remedy, and never seemed to have a doubt in the Infinite Mercy that should cover his infinite guilt.

It was all so orthodox that even if he had doubted (which he did not) the sincerity of the gaoler's contrition and belief, Monsieur the Viscount could have done nothing but envy the easy nature of Antoine's convictions. He forgot the difference of their respective capabilities !

When the night was far advanced the men rose from their knees, and Monsieur the Viscount persuaded Antoine to lie down on his pallet, and when the gaoler's heavy breathing told that he was asleep, Monsieur the Viscount felt relieved to be alone once more; alone, except for Monsieur Crapaud, whose round fiery eyes were open as usual.

The simplicity with which he had been obliged to explain the truths of Divine Love to Antoine, was of signal service to Monsieur the Viscount himself. It left him no excuse for those intricacies of doubt, with which refined minds too often torture themselves; and as he paced feebly up and down the cell, all the long-withheld peace for which he had striven since his imprisonment seemed to flood into his soul. How blessed—how undeservedly blessed—was his fate! Who or what was he that after such short, such mitigated sufferings, the crown of victory should be so near? The way had seemed long to come, it was short to look back upon, and now the golden gates were almost reached, the everlasting doors were open. A few more hours, and then—! and as Monsieur the Viscount buried his worn face in his hands, the tears that trickled from his fingers were literally tears of joy.

He groped his way to the stone, pushed some straw close to it, and lay down on the ground to rest, watched by Monsieur Crapaud's fiery eyes. And as he lay, faces seemed to him to rise out of the darkness, to take the form and features of the face of the Priest, and to gaze at him with unutterable benediction. And in his mind, like some familiar piece of music, awoke the words that had been written on the fly-leaf of the little book; coming back, sleepily and dreamily, over and over again—

" *Souvenez-vous du Sauveur! Souvenez-vous du Sauveur!*"

(Remember the Saviour!)

In that remembrance he fell asleep.

Monsieur the Viscount's sleep for some hours

was without a dream. Then it began to be disturbed by that uneasy consciousness of sleeping too long, which enables some people to awake at whatever hour they have resolved upon. At last it became intolerable, and wearied as he was, he awoke. It was broad daylight, and Antoine was snoring beside him. Surely the cart would come soon, the executions were generally at an early hour. But time went on, and no one came, and Antoine awoke. The hours of suspense passed heavily, but at last there were steps and a key rattled into the lock. The door opened, and the gaoler appeared with a jug of milk and a loaf. With a strange smile he set them down.

"A good appetite to you, citizens."

Antoine flew on him. "Comrade! we used to be friends. Tell me, what is it? Is the execution deferred?"

"The execution has taken place at last," said the other, significantly; "*Robespierre is dead!*" and he vanished.

Antoine uttered a shriek of joy. He wept, he laughed, he cut capers, and flinging himself at Monsieur the Viscount's feet, he kissed them rapturously. When he raised his eyes to Monsieur the Viscount's face, his transports moderated. The last shock had been too much, he seemed almost in a stupor. Antoine got him on to the pallet, dragged the blanket over him, broke the bread into the milk, and played the nurse once more.

On that day thousands of prisoners in the city of Paris alone awoke from the shadow of death to the hope of life. The Reign of Terror was ended!

CHAPTER III.

It was a year of Grace early in the present century.

We are again in the beautiful country of beautiful France. It is the château once more. It is the same, but changed. The unapproachable elegance, the inviolable security, have witnessed invasion. The right wing of the château is in ruins, with traces of fire upon the blackened walls; while here and there, a broken statue or a roofless temple, are sad memorials of the Revolution. Within the restored part of the château, however, all looks well. Monsieur the Viscount has been fortunate, and if not so rich a man as his father, has yet regained enough of his property to live with comfort, and, as he thinks, luxury. The long rooms are little less elegant than in former days, and Madame the present Viscountess's boudoir is a model of taste. Not far from it is another room, to which it forms a singular contrast. This room belongs to Monsieur the Viscount. It is small, with one window. The floors and walls are bare, and it contains no furniture; but on the floor is a worn-out pallet, by which lies a stone, and on that a broken pitcher, and in a little frame against the wall is preserved a crumpled bit of paper like the fly-leaf of some little book, on which is a half-effaced inscription, which can be deciphered by Monsieur the Viscount if by no one else. Above the window is written in large letters, a date and the word REMEMBER. Monsieur the Viscount is not likely to forget, but he is afraid of himself and of prosperity lest it should spoil him.

It is evening, and Monsieur the Viscount is strolling along the terrace with Madame on his arm. He has only one to offer her, for where the other should be an empty sleeve is pinned to his breast, on which a bit of ribbon is stirred by the breeze. Monsieur the Viscount has not been idle since we saw him last; the faith that taught him to die, has taught him also how to live,—an honourable, useful life.

It is evening, and the air comes up perfumed

from a bed of violets by which Monsieur the Viscount is kneeling. Madame (who has a fair face and ashen hair) stands by him with her little hand on his shoulder and her large eyes upon the violets.

"My friend! my friend! my friend!" It is Monsieur the Viscount's voice, and at the sound of it, there is a rustle among the violets that sends the perfume high into the air. Then from the parted leaves come forth first a dirty wrinkled leg, then a dirty wrinkled head with gleaming eyes, and Monsieur Crapaud crawls with self-satisfied dignity on to Monsieur the Viscount's outstretched hand.

So they stay laughing and chatting, and then Monsieur the Viscount bids his friend good-night, and holds him towards Madame, that she may do the same. But Madame (who did not enjoy Monsieur Crapaud's society in prison) cannot be induced to do more than scratch his head delicately with the tip of her white finger. But she respects him greatly, at a distance, she says. Then they go back along the terrace, and are met by a man-servant in Monsieur the Viscount's livery. Is it possible that this is Antoine, with his shock head covered with powder?

Yes; that grating voice which no mental change avails to subdue, is his, and he announces that Monsieur le Curé has arrived. It is the old Curé of the village (who has survived the troubles of the Revolution), and many are the evenings he spends at the château, and many the times in which the closing acts of a noble life are recounted to him, the life of his old friend whom he hopes ere long to see,—of Monsieur the Preceptor. He is kindly welcomed by Monsieur and by Madame, and they pass on together into the château. And when Monsieur the Viscount's steps have ceased to echo from the terrace, Monsieur Crapaud buries himself once more among the violets.

.   .   .   .

Monsieur the Viscount is dead, and Madame sleeps also at his side; and their possessions have descended to their son.

Not the least valued among them, is a case with a glass front and sides, in which, seated upon a stone is the body of a toad stuffed with exquisite skill, from whose head gleam eyes of genuine topaz. Above it in letters of gold is a date, and this inscription :—

"MONSIEUR THE VISCOUNT'S FRIEND."

ADIEU !

Mrs. Alfred Gatty's Popular Works.

" We should not be doing justice to the highest class of juvenile fiction, were we to omit, as particularly worthy of attention at this season, the whole series of Mrs. Gatty's admirable books. They are quite *sui generis*, and deserve the widest possible circulation."—*Literary Churchman.*

PARABLES FROM NATURE; with Notes on the Natural History. Illustrated by W. HOLMAN HUNT, OTTO SPECKTER, C. W. COPE, R.A., E. WARREN, W. MILLAIS, G. THOMAS, and H. CALDERON. 8vo. Ornamental cloth, 10s. 6d. Antique morocco elegant, £1. 1s.

PARABLES FROM NATURE. 16mo. With Illustrations. Tenth Edition. 3s. 6d. Separately: First Series, 1s. 6d.; Second Series, 2s.

RED SNOW, and other Parables from Nature. Third Series, with Illustrations. Second Edition. 16mo. 2s.

WORLDS NOT REALIZED. 16mo. Third Edition. 2s.

PROVERBS ILLUSTRATED. 16mo. With Illustrations. Third Edition. 2s.

⁎ These little works have been found useful for Sunday reading in the family circle, and instructive and interesting to school children.

AUNT JUDY'S TALES. Illustrated by CLARA S. LANE. Fcap. 8vo. Third Edition. 3s. 6d.

AUNT JUDY'S LETTERS. Illustrated by CLARA S. LANE. Fcap. 8vo. 3s. 6d. [*Just published.*

THE HUMAN FACE DIVINE, and other Tales. With Illustrations by C. S. LANE. Fcap. 8vo. 3s. 6d.

THE FAIRY GODMOTHERS, and other Tales. Third Edition. Fcap. 8vo, with Frontispiece. 2s. 6d.

LEGENDARY TALES. With Illustrations by PHIZ. Fcap. 8vo. 5s.

THE POOR INCUMBENT. Fcap. 8vo. Sewed, 1s.; cloth, 1s. 6d.

THE OLD FOLKS FROM HOME; or, A Holiday in Ireland in 1861. Second Edition. Post 8vo. 7s. 6d.

THE LIFE AND ADVENTURES OF RO-
BINSON CRUSOE. By DANIEL DEFOE. With 100
Illustrations by E. H. Wehnert. Uniform with "Ander-
sen's Tales." Small 8vo. Cloth, gilt edges, 7s. 6d.

ANDERSEN'S TALES FOR CHILDREN.
Translated by A. WEHNERT. With 105 Illustrations by
E. H. Wehnert, W. Thomas, and others. Small 8vo.
Cloth, gilt edges, 7s. 6d.

LITTLE MAGGIE AND HER BROTHER.
By Mrs. G. HOOPER, Author of " Recollections of Mrs.
Anderson's School," "Arbell," etc. With a Frontispiece.
Fcap. 8vo. 2s. 6d.

GUESSING STORIES; or, The Surprising
Adventures of the Man with the Extra Pair of Eyes. A
Book for Young People. By a Country Parson. Imperial
16mo. Cloth, gilt edges, 3s.

AMONG THE TARTAR TENTS; or, The
Lost Fathers. A Tale. By ANNE BOWMAN, Author of
" Esperanza," " The Boy Voyagers," etc. With Illustra-
tions. Crown 8vo. 5s.

CAVALIERS AND ROUND-HEADS. By
J. G. EDGAR, Author of " Sea Kings and Naval Heroes."
Illustrated by Amy Butts. Fcap. 8vo. 5s.

SEA-KINGS AND NAVAL HEROES. A
Book for Boys. By J. G. EDGAR. With Illustrations by
C. K. Johnson and C. Keene. Fcap. 8vo. 5s.

THE WHITE LADY AND UNDINE.
Translated from the German by the Hon. C. L. LYTTELTON.
With numerous Illustrations. Fcap. 8vo. 5s.; or, sepa-
rately, 2s. 6d. each.

VERY LITTLE TALES FOR VERY LIT-
TLE CHILDREN. In single Syllables of Four and Five
Letters. New Edition. Illustrated. 2 vols. 16mo. 1s. 6d.
each; or in 1 vol., 3s.

PROGRESSIVE TALES FOR LITTLE
CHILDREN. In words of One and Two Syllables.
Forming the sequel to " Very Little Tales." New Edition.
Illustrated. 2 vols. 16mo. 1s. 6d. each; or in 1 vol., 3s.

THE CHILDREN'S PICTURE-BOOK OF
USEFUL KNOWLEDGE. Written expressly for Young People, and illustrated with 130 Illustrations. Super-royal 16mo. Cloth, gilt edges, 5s.

THE CHILDREN'S PICTURE-BOOK OF
GOOD AND GREAT MEN. Written expressly for Young People, and Illustrated with Fifty large Engravings. Super-royal 16mo. Cloth, gilt edges, 5s. With Coloured Illustrations, 9s.

THE CHILDREN'S PICTURE-BOOK OF
ENGLISH HISTORY. Written expressly for Young People, and Illustrated with Sixty large Engravings. Super-royal 16mo. Cloth, gilt edges, 5s. With Coloured Illustrations, 9s.

THE CHILDREN'S BIBLE PICTURE-
BOOK. Written expressly for Young People, and Illustrated with Eighty large Engravings. Third Edition. Super-royal 16mo. Cloth, gilt edges, 5s. With Coloured Illustrations, 9s.

THE CHILDREN'S PICTURE-BOOK OF
SCRIPTURE PARABLES AND BIBLE MIRACLES, in 1 vol. Cloth, gilt edges, 5s. Coloured, 7s. 6d.

THE CHILDREN'S PICTURE-BOOK OF
SCRIPTURE PARABLES. By the Rev. J. ERSKINE CLARKE. With Sixteen large Illustrations. Super-royal 16mo. Cloth, red edges, 2s. 6d. Coloured, with gilt edges, 3s. 6d.

THE CHILDREN'S PICTURE-BOOK OF
BIBLE MIRACLES. By the Rev. J. ERSKINE CLARKE, M.A. With Sixteen large Illustrations. Super-royal 16mo. Cloth, red edges, 2s. 6d. Coloured, with gilt edges, 3s. 6d.

THE CHILDREN'S BUNYAN'S PIL-
GRIM'S PROGRESS. With Sixteen large Illustrations. New Edition. Super-royal 16mo. Cloth, red edges, 2s. 6d. Coloured, with gilt edges, 3s. 6d.

THE CHILDREN'S PICTURE-BOOK OF
THE LIFE OF JOSEPH, written in Simple Language. With Sixteen large Illustrations. Super-royal 16mo. Cloth, red edges, 2s. 6d. Coloured, with gilt edges, 3s. 6d.

THE LIFE OF CHRISTOPHER COLUM-
BUS, in Short Words. By SARAH CROMPTON. Crown 8vo. 2s. 6d. Also an Edition for Schools, 1s.

THE LIFE OF MARTIN LUTHER, in
Short Words. By the same Author. Crown 8vo. 1s. 6d. Stiff cover, 1s.

THE LIGHTS OF THE WILL O' THE
WISP. Translated by Lady MAXWELL WALLACE. With a coloured Frontispiece. Imperial 16mo. Cloth, gilt edges, 5s.

VOICES FROM THE GREENWOOD.
Adapted from the Original by Lady MAXWELL WALLACE. With Illustrations. Imperial 16mo. 2s. 6d.

PRINCESS ILSE : a Legend ; translated from
the German by Lady MAXWELL WALLACE. With Illustration. Imperial 16mo. 2s. 6d.

REDFIELD ; or, A Visit to the Country. A
Story for Children. With Illustrations by Absolon. Super-royal 16mo. 2s. 6d. Coloured, 3s. 6d.

NURSERY TALES. By Mrs. MOTHERLY.
With Illustrations by C. S. Lane. Imperial 16mo. 2s. 6d. Coloured, gilt edges, 3s. 6d.

NURSERY POETRY. By Mrs. MOTHERLY.
With Eight Illustrations by C. S. Lane. Imperial 16mo. 2s. 6d. Coloured, gilt edges, 3s. 6d.

POETRY FOR PLAY-HOURS. By GERDA
FAY. With Eight large Illustrations. Imperial 16mo. 3s. 6d. Coloured, gilt edges, 4s. 6d.

NURSERY CAROLS. Illustrated with 120
Pictures. By LUDWIG RICHTER and OSCAR PLETSCH. Imperial 16mo. Ornamental binding. 3s. 6d.; coloured, 6s.

A POETRY BOOK FOR CHILDREN. Il-
lustrated with Thirty-seven highly-finished Engravings by C. W. Cope, R.A., Helmsley, Palmer, Skill, Thomas, and H. Weir. New Edition. Crown 8vo. 2s. 6d.

A POETRY BOOK FOR SCHOOLS. With
37 Illustrations. 1s.

MESSRS. BELL AND DALDY'S

NEW AND STANDARD PUBLICATIONS.

𝕹𝖊𝖜 𝕭𝖔𝖔𝖐𝖘.

ERUSALEM Explored; being a Description of the Ancient and Modern City, with upwards of One Hundred Illustrations, consisting of Views, Ground-plans, and Sections. By Dr. Ermete Pierotti, Architect-Engineer to His Excellency Soorraya Pasha of Jerusalem, and Architect of the Holy Land. [*Preparing.*

Plan de Jerusalem Ancienne et Moderne. Par le Docteur Ermete Pierotti. On a large sheet, 41 in. by 29 in.; with numerous details. Price 10s. [*Ready.*

British Seaweeds. Drawn from Professor Harvey's "Phycologia Britannica," with Descriptions by Mrs Alfred Gatty. 4to. [*Shortly.*
This volume contains a drawing of every species of British Seaweed, with magnified sections where necessary, in 803 figures, coloured after nature.

British Moths and Butterflies. Transferred in 195 plates from Curtis's "British Entomology;" with Descriptions by E. W. Janson, Esq., Secretary of the Entomological Society. 4to. [*Shortly.*

British Beetles. Transferred in 259 plates from Curtis's "British Entomology;" with Descriptions by E. W. Janson, Esq., Secretary of the Entomological Society. 4to. [*Shortly.*

The Frithiof Saga. A Poem. Translated from the Norwegian. By the Rev. R. Mucklestone, M.A., Rector of Dinedor, Herefordshire; late Fellow and Tutor of Worcester College, Oxford. Crown 8vo. 7s. 6d.
[*Ready*.

Latin Translations of English Hymns. By Charles Buchanan Pearson, M. A., Prebendary of Sarum, and Rector of Knebworth. Fcap. 8vo. 5s. [*Ready*.

The Book of Common Prayer. Ornamented with Head-pieces and Initial Letters specially designed for this edition. Printed in red and black at the Cambridge University Press. 24mo. Best morocco. 10s. 6d. Also in ornamental bindings, at various prices. [*Ready*.

Also a large paper Edition, crown 8vo. Best morocco, 18s. Also in ornamental bindings, at various prices. [*Ready*.

A Commentary on the Gospels for the Sundays and other Holy Days of the Christian Year. By the Rev. W. Denton, A. M., Worcester College, Oxford; and Incumbent of St. Bartholomew's Cripplegate. Vol. III. [*Preparing*.

Parish Sermons. By the Rev. M. F. Sadler, M.A., Vicar of Bridgwater. Author of the " Sacrament of Responsibility," and " The Second Adam and the New Birth." Fcap. 8vo. Second Series. Trinity to Advent. 7s. 6d. [*Ready*.

Authentic Memoirs of the Christian Church in China. By John Laurence de Mosheim, Chancellor of the University of Göttingen. Translated from the German. Edited, with an Introduction and notes, by Richard Gibbings. B.D., Rector of Tessauran, and Vicar of Ferbane, in the Diocese of Meath. 3s. 6d. [*Ready*.

The Divine Rule of Prayer. By the Rev. R. M. Benson, M.A., Vicar of Cowley, Oxon; Author of " The Wisdom of the Son of David." &c. Fcap. 8vo. [*Shortly*.

Charles and Josiah; or, Friendly Conversations between a Church-man and a Quaker. Crown 8vo. 5s. [*Ready*.

Reasons of Faith; or, the Order of the Christian Argument developed and explained. By the Rev. G. S. Drew, M.A. Fcap. 8vo. 4s. 6d. [*Ready*.

The Book of Psalms; a New Translation, with Introductions and Notes, Critical and Explanatory. By the Rev. J. J. Stewart Perowne, B.D., Fellow of C. C. College, Cambridge, and Examining Chaplain to the Lord Bishop of Norwich. 8vo. [*In the Press*.

The Cotton, Flax, and other Chief Fibre-yielding Plants of India; with a coloured Map of the Country, several original Illustrations of the Native Fibrous Plants, and many important Statistical Tables. By J. Forbes Watson, A.M., M.D., Reporter to the Indian Government on the Products of India. Royal 8vo. [*Immediately*.

Flax and its Products in Ireland. By William Charley, J. P., etc. etc., Juror and Reporter Class XIV, Great Exhibition 1851; also appointed in 1862 for Class XIX. With a Frontispiece. Crown 8vo. 5s.
[*Ready*.

A Handy Book of the Chemistry of Soils : Explanatory of their
Composition, and the Influence of Manures in ameliorating them, with
Outlines of the various Processes of Agricultural Analysis. By John
Scoffern, M.B. Crown 8vo. 4*s.* 6*d.* [*Ready.*

The Thoughts of the Emperor M. Aurelius Antoninus. Translated by George Long. Fcap. 8vo. 6*s.* [*Ready.*

An Old Man's Thoughts about Many Things. Crown 8vo. 7*s.* 6*d.*
[*Ready.*

Hints for Pedestrians, Practical and Medical. By G. C. Watson, M.D. *New Edition.* 2*s.* 6*d.* [*Ready.*

Frederick Lucas. A Biography. By C. J. Riethmüller, author
of " Teuton," a Poem. Crown 8vo. 4*s.* 6*d.* [*Ready.*

Adventures of Baron Wenceslas Wratislaw of Mitrowitz ; what
he saw in the Turkish Metropolis, Constantinople, experienced in his
Captivity, and, [after his happy return to his country, committed to
writing, in the year of our Lord, 1599. Literally translated from the
original Bohemian by A. H. Wratislaw, M.A., Head Master of the
Grammar School, Bury St. Edmunds, and formerly Fellow and Tutor of
Christ's College, Cambridge. Crown 8vo. 6*s.* 6*d.* [*Ready.*

Church Stories. Edited by the Rev. J. E. Clarke. Crown 8vo.
2*s.* 6*d.* [*Ready.*

Aunt Judy's Letters. By Mrs. Alfred Gatty, Author of " Aunt
Judy's Tales," " Parables from Nature," &c. Illustrated by C. S. Lane.
Fcap. 8vo. 3*s.* 6*d.* [*Ready.*

Melchior's Dream, and other Tales. By J. H. G. Edited by
Mrs. Gatty. Illustrated. Fcap. 8vo. 3*s.* 6*d.* [*Ready.*

The Schole Master. By Roger Ascham. Edited by the Rev. J.
E. B. Mayor, M.A. Fcap. 8vo. [*Shortly.*

The Two Addresses of the Hungarian Diet of 1861, to H. I. M.
the Emperor of Austria, with the Imperial Rescript and other Documents. Translated, with Notes, for presentation to Members of both
Houses of Parliament. By J. Horne Payne, Esq., M.A., London, of the
Inner Temple. Royal 8vo. 2*s.* 6*d.* [*Ready.*

The 1862 Edition of Under Government : an Official Key to the
Civil Service, and Guide for Candidates seeking Appointments under the
Crown. By J. C. Parkinson, Inland Revenue, Somerset House. *New
Edition.* Crown 8vo. 3*s.* 6*d.* [*Ready.*

Notes and Queries.—General Index to the Second Series. Fcap.
4to. [*Preparing.*

Gasc's Le Petit Compagnon : a French Talk-book for Little
Children. With numerous woodcuts. 16mo. 2*s.* 6*d.* [*Ready.*

Grammar School Classics. Juvenalis Satirae XVI. With English Notes by Herman Prior, M.A., late Scholar of Trinity College, Oxford. (Expurgated Edition.) Fcap. 8vo. 4*s.* 6*d.* [*Ready.*

Materials for Greek Prose Composition. By the Rev. P. Frost,
M.A., Author of " Materials for Latin Prose Composition." Fcap. 8vo.
Key to ditto. [*Immediately.*

Bell and Daldy's POCKET VOLUMES. A Series of Select Works of Favourite Authors, adapted for general reading, moderate in price, compact and elegant in form, and executed in a style fitting them to be permanently preserved. Imperial 32mo.

Now Ready.

The Robin Hood Ballads. 2s. 6d.
The Midshipman.—Autobiographical Sketches of his own early Career, by Capt. Basil Hall, R.N., F.R.S. From his " Fragments of Voyages and Travels." 3s.
The Lieutenant and Commander. By the same Author. 3s.
Southey's Life of Nelson. 2s. 6d.
George Herbert's Poems. 2s.
George Herbert's Works. 3s.
Longfellow's Poems. 2s. 6d.
Lamb's Tales from Shakspeare. 2s. 6d.
Milton's Paradise Lost. 2s. 6d.
Milton's Paradise Regained and other Poems. 2s. 6d.

Preparing.

White's Natural History of Selborne.
Coleridge's Poems.
The Conquest of India. By Capt. Basil Hall, R.N.
Sea Songs and Ballads. By Charles Dibdin and others.
Walton's Lives of Donne, Wotton, Hooker, &c.
Walton's Complete Angler.
Gray's Poems.
Goldsmith's Poems.
Goldsmith's Vicar of Wakefield.
Henry Vaughan's Poems.
Burns's Poems.
Burns's Songs.
And others.

In cloth, top edge gilt, at 6d. per volume extra ; in half morocco, Roxburgh style, at 1s. extra ; in antique or best plain morocco (Hayday) at 4s. extra.

R. RICHARDSON'S New Dictionary of the English Language. Combining Explanation with Etymology, and copiously illustrated by Quotations from the best authorities. *New Edition,* with a Supplement containing additional Words and further Illustrations. In Two Vols. 4to. 4l. 14s. 6d. Half bound in russia, 5l. 15s. 6d. Russia, 6l. 12s.

The WORDS—with those of the same Family—are traced to their Origin.

The EXPLANATIONS are deduced from the Primitive Meaning through the various Usages.

The QUOTATIONS are arranged Chronologically, from the Earliest Period to the Present Time.

*** The Supplement separately, 4to. 12s.

AN 8VO. EDITION, without the Quotations, 15s. Half-russia, 20s. Russia, 24s.

" It is an admirable addition to our Lexicography, supplying a great desideratum, as exhibiting the biography of each word—its birth, parentage and education, the changes that have befallen it, the company it has kept, and the connexions it has formed—by rich series of quotations, all in chronological order. This is such a Dictionary as perhaps no other language could ever boast."—*Quarterly Review.*

Dr. Richardson on the Study of Language: an Exposition of Horne Tooke's Diversions of Purley. Fcap. 8vo. 4s. 6d.

The Library of English Worthies.

A Series of reprints of the best Authors carefully edited and col-
luted with the Early Copies, and handsomely printed
by Whittingham in Octavo.

GOWER'S Confessio Amantis, with Life by Dr. Pauli,
and a Glossary. 3 vols. 2*l*. 2*s*. Antique calf, 3*l*. 6*s*. Only a
limited number of Copies printed.
   *This important work is so scarce that it can seldom be met
with even in large libraries. It is wanting in nearly every collection of
English Poetry.*

Spenser's Complete Works; with Life, Notes, and Glossary, by
John Payne Collier, Esq., F.S.A. 5 vols. 3*l*. 15*s*. Antique calf, 6*l*. 6*s*.

Bishop Butler's Analogy of Religion; with Analytical Index, by
the Rev. Edward Steere, LL.D. 12*s*. Antique calf, 1*l*. 1*s*.
   " The present edition has been furnished with an Index of the Texts of
Scripture quoted, and an Index of Words and Things considerably fuller
than any hitherto published."—*Editor's Preface.*

Bishop Jeremy Taylor's Rule and Exercises of Holy Living and
Dying. 2 vols. 1*l*. 1*s*. Morocco, antique calf or morocco, 2*l*. 2*s*.

Herbert's Poems and Remains; with S. T. Coleridge's Notes,
and Life by Izaak Walton. Revised, with additional Notes, by Mr. J.
Yeowell. 2 vols. 1*l*. 1*s*. Morocco, antique calf or morocco, 2*l*. 2*s*.

Uniform with the above.

The Physical Theory of Another Life. By Isaac Taylor, Esq.,
Author of " Logic in Theology," " Ultimate Civilization, &c." *New
Edition.* 10*s*. 6*d*. Antique calf, 21*s*.

R. S. W. Singer's New Edition of Shakespeare's Dra-
matic Works. The Text carefully revised, with Notes. The
Life of the Poet and a Critical Essay on each Play by W. W.
Lloyd, Esq. 10 vols. 6*s*. each. Calf, 5*l*. 5*s*. Morocco, 6*l*. 6*s*.
   Large Paper Edition, crown 8vo., 4*l*. 10*s*. Calf, 6*l*. 16*s*. 6*d*.
Morocco, 8*l*. 8*s*.

   " Mr. Singer has produced a text, the accuracy of which cannot be sur-
passed in the present state of antiquarian and philological knowledge."—
Daily News.

The Aldine Edition of the British Poets.

The Publishers have been induced, by the scarcity and increasing value of this admired Series of the Poets, to prepare a New Edition, very carefully corrected, and improved by such additions as recent literary research has placed within their reach.

The general principle of Editing which has been adopted is *to give the entire Poems of each author in strict conformity with the Edition which received his final revision, to prefix a Memoir, and to add such notes as may be necessary to elucidate the sense of obsolete words or explain obscure allusions.* Each author will be placed in the hands of a competent editor specially acquainted with the literature and bibliography of the period.

Externally this new edition will resemble the former, but with some improvements. It will be elegantly printed by Whittingham, on toned paper manufactured expressly for it; and a highly-finished portrait of each author will be given.

The *Aldine Edition of the British Poets* has hitherto been the favourite Series with the admirers of choice books, and every effort will be made to increase its claims as a comprehensive and faithful mirror of the poetic genius of the nation.

AKENSIDE'S Poetical Works, with Memoir by the Rev. A. Dyce, and additional Letters, carefully revised. 5s. Morocco, or antique morocco, 10s. 6d.

Collins's Poems, with Memoir and Notes by W. Moy Thomas, Esq. 3s. 6d. Morocco, or antique morocco, 8s. 6d.

Gray's Poetical Works, with Notes and Memoir by the Rev. John Mitford. 5s. Morocco, or antique morocco, 10s. 6d.

Kirke White's Poems, with Memoir by Sir H. Nicolas, and additional notes. Carefully revised. 5s. Morocco, or antique morocco, 10s. 6d.

Shakespeare's Poems, with Memoir by the Rev. A. Dyce. 5s. Morocco, or antique morocco, 10s. 6d.

Young's Poems, with Memoir by the Rev. John Mitford, and additional Poems. 2 vols. 10s. Morocco, or antique morocco, 1l. 1s.

Thomson's Poems, with Memoir by Sir H. Nicolas, annotated by Peter Cunningham, Esq., F.S.A., and additional Poems, carefully revised. 2 vols. 10s. Morocco, or antique morocco, 1l. 1s.

Thomson's Seasons, and Castle of Indolence, with Memoir. 6s. Morocco, or antique morocco, 11s. 6d.

Dryden's Poetical Works, with Memoir by the Rev. R. Hooper. F.S.A. Carefully revised. [*In the Press.*

Cowper's Poetical Works, including his Translations. Edited, with Memoir, by John Bruce, Esq., F.S.A. [*In the Press.*

Uniform with the Aldine Edition of the Poets.

The Works of Gray, edited by the Rev. John Mitford. With
his Correspondence with Mr. Chute and others, Journal kept at Rome,
Criticism on the Sculptures, &c. *New Edition.* 5 vols. 1*l.* 5*s.*

The Temple and other Poems. By George Herbert, with Coleridge's Notes. *New Edition.* 5*s.* Morocco, antique calf or morocco,
10*s.* 6*d.*

Vaughan's Sacred Poems and Pious Ejaculations, with Memoir
by the Rev. H. F. Lyte. *New Edition.* 5*s.* Antique calf or morocco,
10*s.* 6*d.* *Large Paper,* 7*s.* 6*d.* Antique calf, 14*s.* Antique morocco, 15*s.*
"Preserving all the piety of George Herbert, they have less of his
quaint and fantastic turns, with a much larger infusion of poetic feeling
and expression."—*Lyte.*

Bishop Jeremy Taylor's Rule and Exercises of Holy Living and
Holy Dying. 2 vols. 2*s.* 6*d.* each. Morocco, antique calf or morocco, 7*s.* 6*d.*
each. In one volume, 5*s.* Morocco, antique calf or morocco, 10*s.* 6*d.*

Bishop Butler's Analogy of Religion; with Analytical Introduction and copious Index, by the Rev. Dr. Steere. 6*s.* Antique calf, 11*s.* 6*d.*

Bishop Butler's Sermons and Remains; with Memoir, by the Rev.
E. Steere, LL.D. 6*s.*

•₂ This volume contains some additional remains, which are copyright,
and render it the most complete edition extant.

Bishop Butler's Complete Works; with Memoir by the Rev. Dr.
Steere. 2 vols. 12*s.*

Bacon's Advancement of Learning. Edited, with short Notes,
by the Rev. G. W. Kitchin, M.A., Christ Church, Oxford. 6*s.*; antique
calf, 11*s.* 6*d.*

Bacon's Essays; or, Counsels Civil and Moral, with the Wisdom
of the Ancients. With References and Notes by S. W. Singer, F.S.A. 5*s.*
Morocco, or antique calf, 10*s.* 6*d.*

Bacon's Novum Organum. Newly translated, with short Notes,
by the Rev. Andrew Johnson, M.A. 6*s.* Antique calf, 11*s.* 6*d.*

Locke on the Conduct of the Human Understanding; edited by
Bolton Corney, Esq., M. R. S. L. 3*s.* 6*d.* Antique calf, 8*s.* 6*d.*
"I cannot think any parent or instructor justified in neglecting to put
this little treatise into the hands of a boy about the time when the reason-
ing faculties become developed."—*Hallam.*

Ultimate Civilization. By Isaac Taylor, Esq. 6*s.*

Logic in Theology, and other Essays. By Isaac Taylor, Esq. 6*s.*

The Physical Theory of Another Life. By Isaac Taylor, Esq.,
Author of the "Natural History of Enthusiasm," "Restoration of Belief,"
&c. *New Edition.* 6*s.* Antique calf, 11*s.* 6*d.*

OMESTIC Life in Palestine. By M. E. Rogers. Post
8vo. 10s. 6d.

By-Roads and Battle Fields in Picardy: with Inci-
dents and Gatherings by the Way between Ambleteuse and
Ham; including Agincourt and Crécy. By G. M. Musgrave, M.A.,
Author of "A Pilgrimage into Dauphiné, &c. Illustrated. Super-
royal 8vo. 16s.

The Boat and the Caravan. A Family Tour through Egypt and
Syria. *New and cheaper Edition.* Fcap. 8vo. 5s. 6d.

Fragments of Voyages and Travels. By Captain Basil Hall,
R.N., F.R.S. 1st, 2nd, and 3rd Series in 1 vol. complete. *New Edition.*
Royal 8vo. 10s. 6d.

The Gem of Thorney Island; or, The Historical Associations of
Westminster Abbey. By the Rev. J. Ridgway, M.A. Crown 8vo. 7s. 6d.

The Life and Times of Aonio Paleario; or, a History of the
Italian Reformers in the Sixteenth Century. Illustrated by Original
Letters and unedited Documents. By M. Young. 2 vols. 8vo. 1l. 12s.

Gifts and Graces. A new Tale, by the Author of "The Rose and
the Lotus." Post 8vo. 7s. 6d.

Childhood and Youth. By Count Nicola Tolstoi. Translated
from the Russian by Malwida von Meysenbug. Post 8vo. 8s. 6d.

Baronscliffe; or, the Deed of other Days. By Mrs. P. M.
Latham, Author of "The Wayfarers." Crown 8vo. 6s.

The Wayfarers: or, Toil and Rest. By Mrs. Latham. Fcap. 5s.

The Manse of Mastland. Sketches: Serious and Humorous, in
the Life of a Village Pastor in the Netherlands. Translated from the
Dutch by Thomas Keightley, M.A. Post 8vo. 9s.

The Home Life of English Ladies in the Seventeenth Century.
By the Author of "Magdalen Stafford." *Second Edition, enlarged.*
Fcap. 8vo. 6s. Calf, 9s. 6d.

The Romance and its Hero. By the Author of "Magdalen Stafford." 2 vols. Fcap. 8vo. 12s.

Magdalen Stafford. A Tale. Fcap. 8vo. 5s.

Claude de Vesci; or, the Lost Inheritance. 2 vols. Fcap. 8vo. 9s.

Maud Bingley. By Frederica Graham. 2 vols. Fcap. 8vo. 12s.

BY THE LATE MRS. WOODROOFFE.

OTTAGE Dialogues. *New Edition.* 12mo. 4s. 6d.

Shades of Character; or, the Infant Pilgrim. 7th Edition.
2 vols. 12mo. 12s.

Michael Kemp, the Happy Farmer's Lad. 8th Edition. 12mo. 4s.

A Sequel to Michael Kemp. *New Edition.* 12mo. 6s. 6d.

MRS. ALFRED GATTY'S POPULAR WORKS.

" We should not be doing justice to the highest class of juvenile fiction, were we to omit, as particularly worthy of attention at this season, the whole series of Mrs. Gatty's admirable books. They are quite *sui generis*, and deserve the widest possible circulation."—*Literary Churchman.*

ARABLES from Nature; with Notes on the Natural History. Illustrated by W. Holman Hunt, Otto Speckter, C. W. Cope, R. A., E. Warren, W. Millais, G. Thomas, and H. Calderon. 8vo. Ornamental cloth, 10s. 6d. Antique morocco elegant, 1l. 1s.

Parables from Nature. 16mo. with Illustrations. *Tenth Edition.* 3s. 6d. Separately: First Series, 1s. 6d.; Second Series, 2s.

Red Snow, and other Parables from Nature. Third Series, with Illustrations. *Second Edition.* 16mo. 2s.

Worlds not Realized. 16mo. *Third Edition.* 2s.

Proverbs Illustrated. 16mo. with Illustrations. 3rd *Edition.* 2s.

* These little works have been found useful for Sunday reading in the family circle, and instructive and interesting to school children.

The Human Face Divine, and other Tales. With Illustrations by C. S. Lane. Fcap. 8vo. 3s. 6d.

The Fairy Godmothers and other Tales. *Third Edition.* Fcap. 8vo. with Frontispiece. 2s. 6d.

Legendary Tales. With Illustrations by Phiz. Fcap. 8vo. 5s.

The Poor Incumbent. Fcap. 8vo. Sewed, 1s. Cloth, 1s. 6d.

The Old Folks from Home; or, a Holiday in Ireland in 1861. *Second Edition.* Post 8vo. 7s. 6d.

Aunt Judy's Tales. Illustrated by Clara S. Lane. Fcap. 8vo. *Third Edition.* 3s. 6d.

Aunt Judy's Letters. Illustrated by Clara S. Lane. Fcap. 8vo. 3s. 6d. [*Just published.*

Melchior's Dream, and other Tales. By J. H. G. Edited by Mrs. Gatty. Illustrated. Fcap. 8vo. 3s. 6d. [*Just published.*

HE Life and Adventures of Robinson Crusoe. By Daniel Defoe. With 100 Illustrations by E. H. Wehnert. Uniform with "Andersen'sTales." Small 8vo. Cloth, gilt edges, 7s. 6d.

Andersen's Tales for Children. Translated by A. Wehnert. With 105 Illustrations by E. H. Wehnert, W. Thomas, and others. Small 8vo. Cloth, gilt edges, 7s. 6d.

Among the Tartar Tents; or, the Lost Fathers. A Tale By Anne Bowman, Author of " Esperanza," " The Boy Voyagers," &c. With Illustrations. Crown 8vo 5s.

Little Maggie and her Brother. By Mrs. G. Hooper, Author of " Recollections of Mrs. Anderson's School," " Arbell," &c. With a Frontispiece. Fcap. 8vo. 2s. 6d.

A 2

Guessing Stories; or, the Surprising Adventures of the Man with the Extra Pair of Eyes. A Book for Young People. By a Country Parson. Imperial 16mo. Cloth, gilt edges, 3s.

Cavaliers and Round Heads. By J. G. Edgar, Author of " Sea Kings and Naval Heroes." Illustrated by Amy Butts. Fcap. 8vo. 5s.

Sea-Kings and Naval Heroes. A Book for Boys. By J. G. Edgar. With Illustrations by C. K. Johnson and C. Keene. Fcap. 8vo. 5s.

The Life of Christopher Columbus, in Short Words. By Sarah Crompton. Crown 8vo. 2s. 6d. Also an Edition for Schools, 1s.

The Life of Martin Luther, in Short Words. By the same Author. Crown 8vo. 1s. 6d. Stiff cover, 1s.

Redfield; or, a Visit to the Country. A Story for Children. With Illustrations by Absolon. Super royal 16mo. 2s. 6d. Coloured, 3s. 6d.

Nursery Tales. By Mrs. Motherly. With Illustrations by C. S. Lane. Imperial 16mo. 2s. 6d. Coloured, gilt edges, 3s. 6d.

Nursery Poetry. By Mrs. Motherly. With Eight Illustrations by C. S. Lane. Imperial 16mo. 2s. 6d. Coloured, gilt edges, 3s. 6d.

Nursery Carols. Illustrated with 120 Pictures. By Ludwig Riether and Oscar Pletsch. Imperial 16mo. Ornamental Binding. 3s. 6d. coloured, 6s.

Poetry for Play-Hours. By Gerda Fay. With Eight large Illustrations. Imperial 16mo. 3s. 6d. Coloured, gilt edges, 4s. 6d.

Very Little Tales for Very Little Children In single Syllables of *Four* and *Five* letters. *New Edition.* Illustrated. 2 vols. 16mo. 1s. 6d. each, or in 1 vol. 3s.

Progressive Tales for Little Children. In words of *One* and *Two* Syllables. Forming the sequel to " Very Little Tales." *New Edition.* Illustrated. 2 vols. 16mo. 1s. 6d. each, or in 1 vol. 3s.

The White Lady and Undine, translated from the German by the Hon. C. L. Lyttelton. With numerous Illustrations. Fcap. 8vo. 5s. Or, separately, 2s. 6d. each.

The Lights of the Will o' the Wisp. Translated by Lady Maxwell Wallace. With a coloured Frontispiece. Imperial 16mo. Cloth, gilt edges, 5s.

Voices from the Greenwood. Adapted from the Original. By Lady Maxwell Wallace. With Illustrations. Imperial 16mo. 2s. 6d.

Princess Ilse: a Legend, translated from the German. By Lady Maxwell Wallace. With Illustrations. Imperial 16mo. 2s. 6d.

A Poetry Book for Children. Illustrated with Thirty-seven highly-finished Engravings, by C. W. Cope, R. A., Helmsley, Palmer, Skill, Thomas, and H. Weir. *New Edition.* Crown 8vo. 2s. 6d.

The Children's Picture Book Series.

Written expressly for Young People, super-royal 16mo.

Cloth, gilt edges, price 5s. each.

BIBLE Picture Book. Eighty Illustrations. (Coloured, 9s.)

Scripture Parables and Bible Miracles. Thirty-two Illustrations. (Coloured, 7s. 6d.)

English History. Sixty Illustrations. (Coloured, 9s.)

Good and Great Men. Fifty Illustrations. (Coloured, 9s.)

Useful Knowledge. One Hundred and Thirty Illustrations.

Cloth, red edges, price 2s. 6d. each. (Coloured, gilt edges, 3s. 6d.)

Scripture Parables. By the Rev. J. Erskine Clarke. Sixteen Illustrations.

Bible Miracles. By the Rev. J. Erskine Clarke, M.A. Sixteen Illustrations.

The Life of Joseph. Sixteen Illustrations.

Bunyan's Pilgrim's Progress. Sixteen Illustrations.

CLARK'S Introduction to Heraldry.—Containing Rules for Blazoning and Marshalling Coats of Armour—Dictionary of Terms—Orders of Knighthood explained—Degrees of the Nobility and Gentry—Tables of Precedency; 48 Engravings, including upwards of 1,000 Examples, and the Arms of numerous Families. *Sixteenth Edition improved.* Small 8vo. 7s. 6d. Coloured, 18s.

Book of Family Crests and Mottoes, with *Four Thousand Engravings* of the Crests of the Peers, Baronets, and Gentry of England and Wales, and Scotland and Ireland. A Dictionary of Mottos, &c. *Ninth Edition, enlarged.* 2 vols. small 8vo. 1l. 1s.

" Perhaps the best recommendation to its utility and correctness (in the main) is, that it has been used as a work of reference in the Heralds College. No wonder it sells."—*Spectator.*

Book of Mottoes, used by the Nobility, Gentry, &c. with Translations, &c. *New Edition, enlarged.* Small 8vo. cloth gilt, 2s. 6d.

A Handbook of Mottoes borne by the Nobility, Gentry, Cities, Public Companies, &c. Translated and Illustrated, with Notes and Quotations, by C. N. Elvin, M.A. Small 8vo. 6s.

Gothic Ornaments; being a Series of Examples of enriched Details and Accessories of the Architecture of Great Britain. Drawn from existing Authorities. By J. K. Colling, Architect. Royal 4to. Vol. I. 3l. 13s. 6d. Vol. II. 3l. 16s. 6d.

Details of Gothic Architecture, Measured and Drawn from existing Examples. By J. K. Colling, Architect. Royal 4to. 2 vols. 5*l*. 5*s*.

The Architectural History of Chichester Cathedral, with an Introductory Essay on the Fall of the Tower and Spire. By the Rev. R. Willis, M.A., F.R.S., &c., Jacksonian Professor in the University of Cambridge.—Of Boxgrove Priory, by the Rev. J. L. Petit, M.A., F.S.A. —And of Shoreham Collegiate Church, together with the Collective Architectural History of the foregoing buildings, as indicated by their mouldings, by Edmund Sharpe, M.A., F.R.I B.A. Illustrated by one hundred Plates, Diagrams, Plans and Woodcuts. Super-royal 4to. 1*l*. 10*s*.

Architectural Studies in France. By the Rev. J. L. Petit, M.A., F.S.A. With Illustrations from Drawings by the Author and P. H. Delamotte. Imp. 8vo. 2*l*. 2*s*.

Remarks on Church Architecture. With Illustrations. By the Rev. J. L. Petit, M.A. 2 vols. 8vo. 1*l*. 1*s*.

Lectures on Church Building : with some Practical Remarks on Bells and Clocks. By E. B. Denison, M.A. *Second Edition.* Rewritten and enlarged ; with Illustrations. Crown 8vo. 7*s*. 6*d*.

A Few Notes on the Temple Organ. By Edmund Macrory, M.A. *Second Edition* Super-royal 16mo. Half morocco, Roxburgh, 3*s*. 6*d*.

Scudamore Organs, or Practical Hints respecting Organs for Village Churches and small Chancels, on improved principles. By the Rev. John Baron, M.A., Rector of Upton Scudamore, Wilts. With Designs by George Edmund Street, F.S.A. *Second Edition, revised and enlarged.* 8vo. 6*s*.

Memoirs of Musick. By the Hon. Roger North, Attorney-General to James II. Now first printed from the original MS., and edited, with copious Notes, by Dr. E. F. Rimbault. Fcap. 4to. half morocco, 1*l*. 10*s*.

The Bell; its Origin, History, and Uses. By Rev. A. Gatty. 3*s*.

Practical Remarks on Belfries and Ringers. By the Rev. H. T. Ellacombe, M.A., F.A.S., Rector of Clyst St. George, Devonshire. *Second Edition*, with an Appendix on Chiming. Illustrated. 8vo. 3*s*.

Proceedings of the Archæological Institute at Newcastle, in 1853. With Numerous Engravings. 2 vols. 8vo. 2*l*. 2*s*.

History of the Parish of Ecclesfield, in the County of York. By the Rev. J. Eastwood, M.A., Incumbent of Hope, Staffordshire, formerly Curate of Ecclesfield. 8vo. 16*s*.

A Handbook for Visitors to Cambridge. By Norris Deck. Illustrated by 8 Steel Engravings, 97 Woodcuts, and a Map. Crown 8vo. 5*s*.

Canterbury in the Olden Time: from the Municipal Archives and other Sources. By John Brent, F.S.A. With Illustrations. 5*s*.

Whirlwinds and Dust-Storms of India. With numerous Illustrations drawn from Nature, bound separately; and an Addendum on Sanitary Measures required for European Soldiers in India. By P. F. H. Baddeley, Surgeon, Bengal Army, Retired List. Large 8vo. With Illustrations, 8*s*. 6*d*.; without Illustrations, 3*s*.
   Two Transparent Wind Cards in Horn, adapted to the Northern and Southern Hemispheres, for the use of Sailors. 2*s*.

EBSTER'S Complete Dictionary of the English Language. *New Edition*, revised and greatly enlarged, by CHAUNCEY A. GOODRICH, Professor in Yale College. 4to. (1624 pp.) 1*l.* 11*s.* 6*d.*; half calf, 2*l.*; calf, or half russia, 2*l.* 2*s.*; russia, 2*l.* 10*s.*

Though the circulation of Dr. Webster's celebrated Dictionary, in it various forms, in the United States, in England, and in every country where the English Language is spoken, may be counted by hundreds of thousands, it is believed that there are many persons to whom the book is yet unknown, and who, if seeking for a Dictionary which should supply all reasonable wants, would be at a loss to select one from the numerous competitors in the field.

In announcing this New Edition, the Proprietors desire to call attention to the features which distinguish it, and to put before those who are in want of such a book, the points in which it excels all other Dictionaries, and which render it the best that has as yet been issued for the practical purposes of daily use :—
1. Accuracy of Definition. 2. Pronunciation intelligibly marked. 3. Completeness. 4. Etymology. 5. Obsolete Words. 6. Uniformity in the Mode of Spelling. 7. Quotations. 8. Cheapness.

With the determination that the superiority of the work shall be fully maintained, and that it shall keep pace with the requirements of the age and the universal increase of education, the Proprietors have added to this New Edition, under the editorship of Professor Goodrich,—

A Table of Synonyms. An Appendix of New Words. Table of Quotations, Words, Phrases, &c.

Tables of Interest, enlarged and Improved; calculated at Five per Cent.; Showing at one view the Interest of any Sum, from £1 to £365: they are also carried on by hundreds to £1,000, and by thousands to £10,000, from one day to 365 days. To which are added, Tables of Interest, from one to 12 months, and from two to 13 years. Also Tables for calculating Commission on Sales of Goods or Banking Accounts, from ⅛ to 5 per Cent., with several useful additions, among which are Tables for calculating Interest on large sums for 1 day, at the several rates of 4 and 5 per Cent. to £100,000,000. By Joseph King, of Liverpool. 24*th Edition*. With a Table showing the number of days from any one day to any other day in the Year. 8vo. 1*l.* 1*s.*

EGENDS and Lyrics, by Adelaide Anne Procter. 6*th Edition*. Fcap. 5*s.* Antique or best plain morocco, 10*s.* 6*d.*

—— *Second Series. Second Edition.* Fcap. 8vo. 5*s.*; antique or best plain morocco, 10*s.* 6*d.*

The Legend of the Golden Prayers, and other Poems. By C. F. Alexander, Author of "Moral Songs," &c. Fcap. 8vo. 5*s.*; antique or best plain morocco, 10*s.* 6*d.*

Verses for Holy Seasons. By the Same Author. Edited by the Very Rev. W. F. Hook, D.D. 4*th Edition*. Fcap. 3*s.* 6*d.*; morocco, antique calf or morocco, 8*s.* 6*d.*

Nightingale Valley : a Collection of the Choicest Lyrics and Short Poems in the English Language. Fcap. 8vo. 5*s.*; morocco, antique calf or morocco, 10*s.* 6*d.*

Saul, a Dramatic Poem ; Elizabeth, an Historical Ode; and other Poems. By William Fulford, M.A. Fcap. 8vo. 5*s.*

Lays and Poems on Italy. By F. A. Mackay. Fcap. 8vo. 5s.

Poems from the German. By Richard Garnett, Author of " Io in Egypt, and other Poems." Fcap. 8vo. 3s. 6d.

Io in Egypt, and other Poems. By R. Garnett. Fcap. 8vo. 5s.

The Monks of Kilcrea, and other Poems. *Third Edition.* Post 8vo. 7s. 6d.

Christopheros, and other Poems. By the Ven. W. B. Mant, Archdeacon of Down. Crown 8vo. 6s.

Teuton. A Poem. By C. J. Riethmüller. Crown 8vo. 7s. 6d.

Dryope, and other Poems. By T. Ashe. Fcap. 8vo. 6s.

Poems. By Thomas Ashe. Fcap. 8vo. 5s.

Day and Night Songs and The Music Master, a Love Poem. By William Allingham. With Nine Illustrations. Fcap. 8vo. 6s. 6d.; morocco, 11s. 6d.

Wild Thyme. By E. M. Mitchell. Fcap. 8vo. 5s.

Lyrics and Idylls. By Gerda Fay. Fcap. 8vo. 4s.

Pansies. By Fanny Susan Wyvill. Fcap. 8vo. 5s.

The Defence of Guenevere, and other Poems. By W. Morris. 5s.

David Mallet's Poems. With Notes and Illustrations by F. Dinsdale, LL.D., F.S.A. *New Edition.* Post 8vo. 10s. 6d.

Ballads and Songs of Yorkshire. Transcribed from private MSS., rare Broadsides, and scarce Publications; with Notes and a Glossary. By C. J. D. Ingledew, M.A., Ph.D., F.G.H.S., author of " The History of North Allerton." Fcap. 8vo. 6s.

Passion Week. By the Editor of " Christmas Tyde." With 16 Illustrations from Albert Durer. Imp. 16mo. 7s. 6d.; antique morocco, 14s.

Percy's Reliques of Ancient English Poetry. 3 vols. sm. 8vo. 15s. Half-bound, 18s. Antique calf, or morocco, 1l. 11s. 6d.

Ellis's Specimens of Early English Poetry. 3 vols. sm. 8vo. 15s. Half-bound, 18s. Antique calf, or morocco, 1l. 11s. 6d.

The Book of Ancient Ballad Poetry of Great Britain, Historical, Traditional and Romantic: with Modern Imitations, Translations, Notes and Glossary, &c. Edited by J. S. Moore. *New and Improved Edition,* 8vo. Half-bound, 14s. Antique morocco, 21s.

Shakespeare's Tempest. With Illustrations by Birket Foster, Gustave Doré, Frederick Skill, Alfred Slader, and Gustave Janet. Crown 4to. Ornamental cloth, 10s. 6d. Antique morocco elegant, 1l. 1s.

The Promises of Jesus Christ. Illuminated by Albert H. Warren, *Second Edition.* Ornamental cloth, 15s. Antique morocco elegant, 21s.

Christmas with the Poets : a Collection of English Poetry relating to the Festival of Christmas. Illustrated by Birket Foster, and with numerous initial letters and borders beautifully printed in gold and colours by Edmund Evans. *New and improved Edition.* Super royal 8vo. Ornamental binding, 21s. Antique morocco, 31s. 6d.

THENÆ Cantabrigienses. By C. H. Cooper, F.S.A., and Thompson Cooper. Volume I. 1500—1585. 8vo. 18*s.* Vol. II. 1586—1609. 8vo. 18*s.*

This work, in illustration of the biography of notable and eminent men who have been members of the University of Cambridge, comprehends notices of:—1. Authors. 2. Cardinals, archbishops, bishops, abbots, heads of religious houses and other church dignitaries. 3. Statesmen, diplomatists, military and naval commanders. 4. Judges and eminent practitioners of the civil or common law. 5. Sufferers for religious or political opinions. 6. Persons distinguished for success in tuition. 7. Eminent physicians and medical practitioners. 8. Artists, musicians, and heralds. 9. Heads of colleges, professors, and principal officers of the university. 10. Benefactors to the university and colleges, or to the public at large.

The Early and Middle Ages of England. By C. H. Pearson, M.A., Fellow of Oriel College, Oxford, and Professor of Modern History, King's College, London. 8vo. 12*s.*

History of England, from the Invasion of Julius Cæsar to the End of the Reign of George II., by Hume and Smollett. With the Continuation, to the Accession of Queen Victoria, by the Rev. T. S. Hughes, B.D. late Canon of Peterborough. *New Edition,* containing Historical Illustrations, Autographs, and Portraits, copious Notes, and the Author's last Corrections and Improvements. In 18 vols. crown 8vo. 4*s.* each.

> Vols. I. to VI. (Hume's portion), 1*l.* 4*s.*
> Vols. VII. to X. (Smollett's ditto), 16*s.*
> Vols. XI. to XVIII. (Hughes's ditto), 1*l.* 12*s.*

History of England, from the Accession of George III. to the Accession of Queen Victoria. By the Rev. T. S. Hughes, B.D. *New Edition,* almost entirely re-written. In 7 vols. 8vo. 3*l.* 13*s.* 6*d.*

Choice Notes from " Notes and Queries," by the Editor. Fcap. 8vo. 5*s.* each.
> Vol. I.—History. Vol. II.—Folk Lore.

Master Wace's Chronicle of the Conquest of England. Translated from the Norman by Sir Alexander Malet, Bart., H.B.M. Plenipotentiary, Frankfort. With Photograph Illustrations of the Bayeaux Tapestry. Medium 4to. Half-morocco, Roxburgh, 2*l.* 2*s.*

The Prince Consort's Addresses on Different Public Occasions. Beautifully printed by Whittingham. 4to. 10*s.* 6*d.*

Life and Books; or, Records of Thought and Reading. By J. F. Boyes, M.A. Fcap. 8vo. 5*s.*; calf, 8*s.* 6*d.*

Life's Problems. *Second Edition,* revised and enlarged. Fcap. 5*s.*

Parliamentary Short-Hand (Official System). By Thompson Cooper. Fcap. 8vo. 2*s.* 6*d.*

This is the system *universally practised by the Government Official Reporters.* It has many advantages over the system ordinarily adopted, and has hitherto been inaccessible, except in a high-priced volume.

English Retraced; or, Remarks, Critical and Philological, founded on a Comparison of the Breeches Bible with the English of the present day. Crown 8vo. 5*s.*

The Pleasures of Literature. By R. Aris Willmott, Incumbent of Bear-Wood. *Fifth Edition*, enlarged. Fcap. 8vo. 5s. Morocco, 10s. 6d.

Hints and Helps for Youths leaving School. By the Rev. J. S. Gilderdale, M.A. Fcap. 8vo. 5s. Calf, 8s. 6d.

Hints to Maid Servants in Small Households, on Manners, Dress, and Duties. By Mrs. Motherly. Fcap. 8vo. 1s. 6d.

A Wife's Home Duties; containing Hints to inexperienced Housekeepers. Fcap. 8vo. 2s. 6d.

Geology in the Garden: or, The Fossils in the Flint Pebbles. With 106 Illustrations. By the Rev. Henry Eley, M.A. Fcap. 8vo. 6s.

Halcyon: or Rod-Fishing in Clear Waters. By Henry Wade, Secretary to the Weardale Angling Association. With Coloured representations of the principal Flies, and other Illustrations. Cr. 8vo. 7s. 6d.

SERMONS.

ARISH SERMONS. By the Rev. M. F. Sadler, M.A., Vicar of Bridgwater. Author of the " Sacrament of Responsibility," and " The Second Adam and the New Birth." Vol. I. Advent to Trinity. Fcap. 8vo. 7s. 6d.

Twenty-four Sermons on Christian Doctrine and Practice, and on the Church. By C. J. Blomfield, D.D., late Lord Bishop of London. (*Hitherto unpublished.*) 8vo. 10s. 6d.

King's College Sermons. By the Rev. E. H. Plumptre, M.A., Divinity Professor. Fcap. 8vo. 2s. 6d.

Sermons preached in Westminster. By the Rev. C. F. Secretan, M.A., Incumbent of Holy Trinity, Vauxhall-Bridge Road. Fcap. 8vo. 6s.

Sermons. By the Rev. A. Gatty, D.D., Vicar of Ecclesfield. 12mo. 8s.

Twenty Plain Sermons for Country Congregations and Family Reading. By the Rev. A. Gatty, D.D., Vicar of Ecclesfield. Fcap. 5s.

Sermons to a Country Congregation—Advent to Trinity. By the Rev. Hastings Gordon, M.A. 12mo 6s.

Sermons on Popular Subjects, preached in the Collegiate Church, Wolverhampton. By the Rev. Julius Lloyd, M.A. 8vo. 4s. 6d.

Gospel Truths in Parochial Sermons for the Great Festivals. By the Rev. J. Townson, M.A. Fcap. 8vo. 2s. 6d.

Four Sermons on the " Comfortable Words" in the Office for the Holy Communion. By Alexander Goalen, B.A. Fcap. 8vo. 2s.

The Prodigal Son. Sermons by W. R. Clark, M.A., Vicar of Taunton, S. Mary Magdalene. Fcap. 8vo. 2s. 6d.

Parochial Sermons. By the Rev. D. G. Stacy, Vicar of Hornchurch, Essex. Fcap. 8vo. 5s.

Sermons Suggested by the Miracles of our Lord and Saviour Jesus Christ. By the Very Rev. Dean Hook. 2 vols. Fcap. 8vo. 12s.

Five Sermons Preached before the University of Oxford. By the Very Rev. W. F. Hook, D.D., Dean of Chichester. *Third Edition.* 3s.

Plain Parochial Sermons. By the Rev. C. F. C. Pigott, B.A., late Curate of St. Michael's, Handsworth. Fcap. 8vo. 6s.

Our Privileges, Responsibilities, and Trials. By the Rev. E. Phillips, M.A. Fcap. 8vo. 5s.

Sermons, chiefly Practical. By the Rev. T. Nunns, M. A. Edited by the Very Rev. W. F. Hook, D.D., Dean of Chichester. Fcap. 8vo. 6s.

Sermons, Preached in the Parish Church of Godalming, Surrey, by the Rev. E. J. Boyce, M.A., Vicar. *Second Edition.* Fcap. 8vo. 6s.

Life in Christ. By the Rev. J. Llewellyn Davies, M.A., Rector of Christ Church, Marylebone. Fcap. 8vo. 5s.

The Bible and its Interpreters: being the Substance of Three Sermons preached in the Parish Church, St. Ann, Wandsworth. By James Booth, LL.D., Vicar of Stone, Buckinghamshire. 8vo. 2s. 6d.

The Church of England; its Constitution, Mission, and Trials. By the Rt. Rev. Bishop Broughton. Edited, with a Prefatory Memoir, by the Ven. Archdeacon Harrison. 8vo. 10s. 6d.

Plain Sermons, Addressed to a Country Congregation. By the late E. Blencowe, M.A. 1st and 3rd Series, fcap. 8vo. 7s. 6d. each.

Occasional Sermons. By a Member of the Church of England. Fcap. 8vo. 2s. 6d.

Missionary Sermons preached at Hagley. Fcap. 3s. 6d.

The Sufficiency of Christ. Sermons preached during the Reading Lenten Mission of 1860. Fcap. 8vo. 2s. 6d.

Westminster Abbey Sermons for the Working Classes. Fcap. *Authorized Edition.* 1858. 2s.: 1859. 2s. 6d.

Sermons preached at St. Paul's Cathedral. *Authorized Edition.* 1859. Fcap. 8vo. 2s. 6d.

AILY Readings for a Year, on the Life of Our Lord and Saviour Jesus Christ. By the Rev. Peter Young, M.A. *Second Edition*, improved. 2 vols. Crown 8vo. 1l. 1s. Antique calf, 1l. 16s. Morocco, Hayday, 2l.

A Commentary on the Gospels for the Sundays and other Holy Days of the Christian Year. By the Rev. W. Denton, A.M., Worcester College, Oxford, and Incumbent of St. Bartholomew's, Cripplegate. 8vo. Vol. 1. Advent to Easter, 15s. Vol. II. Easter to the Sixteenth Sunday after Trinity, 14s.

Short Sunday Evening Readings, Selected and Abridged from various Authors by the Dowager Countess of Cawdor. In large type. 8vo. 5s.

Lights of the Morning: or, Meditations for every Day in the Year. From the German of Frederic Arndt. With a Preface by the Rev. W. C. Magee, D. D. Fcap. 8vo. Advent to Whitsuntide, 5s. 6d. Trinity, 5s. 6d.

The Second Adam, and the New Birth; or, the Doctrine of Baptism as contained in Holy Scripture. By the Rev. M. F. Sadler, M.A. Vicar of Bridgewater, Author of "The Sacrament of Responsibility." *Third Edition*, greatly enlarged. Fcap. 8vo. 4s. 6d.

The Sacrament of Responsibility; or, Testimony of the Scripture to the teaching of the Church on Holy Baptism, with especial reference to the Cases of Infants, and Answers to Objections. *Sixth Edition*. 6d.

Popular Illustrations of some Remarkable Events recorded in the Old Testament. By the Rev. J. F. Dawson, LL.B., Rector of Toynton. Post 8vo. 8s. 6d.

The Acts and Writings of the Apostles. By C. Pickering Clarke, M.A., late Curate of Teddington. Post 8vo. Vol. I., with Map., 7s. 6d.

The Spirit of the Hebrew Poetry. By Isaac Taylor, Esq., Author of "The Natural History of Enthusiasm," "Ultimate Civilization," &c. 8vo. 10s. 6d.

The Wisdom of the Son of David: an Exposition of the First Nine Chapters of the Book of Proverbs. Fcap. 8vo. 5s.

A Companion to the Authorized Version of the New Testament: being Explanatory Notes, together with Explanatory Observations and an Introduction. By the Rev. H. B. Hall, B.C.L. *Second and cheaper Edition*, revised and enlarged. Fcap. 8vo. 3s. 6d.

A History of the Church of England from the Accession of James II. to the Rise of the Bangorian Controversy in 1717. By the Rev. T. Debary, M.A. 8vo. 14s.

A Treatise on Metaphysics in Connexion with Revealed Religion. By the Rev. J. H. MacMahon. 8vo. 14s.

Aids to Pastoral Visitation, selected and arranged by the Rev. H. B. Browning, M.A., Curate of St. George, Stamford. 8vo. 5s.

A Popular Paraphrase of St. Paul's Epistle to the Romans, with Notes. By the Rev. A. C. Bromehead, M.A. Crown 8vo. 3s. 6d.

Remarks on Certain Offices of the Church of England, popularly termed the Occasional Services. By the Rev. W. J. Dampier. 12mo. 5s.

The Sympathy of Christ. Six Readings for the Sundays in Lent, or for the Days of the Holy Week. By the Rev. W. J. Dampier, M.A., Vicar of Coggeshall. *Second Edition*. 18mo. 2s. 6d.

On Party Spirit in the English Church. By the Rev. S. Robins. 12mo. 2s. 6d.

Papers on Preaching and Public Speaking. By a Wykehamist.
Fcap. 8vo. 5s.
This volume is an enlargement and extension, with corrections, of the Papers which appeared in the " Guardian " in 1858-9.

The Speaker at Home. Chapters on Public Speaking and Reading
aloud, by the Rev. J. J. Halcombe, M.A., and on the Physiology of Speech, by W. H. Stone, M.A., M.B. *Second Edition.* Fcap. 8vo. 3s. 6d.

The English Churchman's Signal. By the Writer of " A Plain
Word to the Wise in Heart." Fcap. 8vo. 2s. 6d.

A Plain Word to the Wise in Heart on our Duties at Church, and
on our Prayer Book. *Fourth Edition.* Sewed, 1s. 6d.

Register of Parishioners who have received Holy Confirmation.
Arranged by William Fraser, B. C. L., Vicar of Alton. Oblong 4to. 7s. 6d.; 10s. 6d.; 12s.

Readings on the Morning and Evening Prayer and the Litany.
By J. S. Blunt. *Second Edition, enlarged.* Fcap. 8vo. 3s. 6d.

Confirmation. By J. S. Blunt, Author of " Readings on the
Morning and Evening Prayer," &c. Fcap. 8vo. 3s. 6d.

Life after Confirmation. By the same Author. 18mo. 1s.

The Book of Psalms (Prayer Book Version). With Short Head-
ings and Explanatory Notes. By the Rev. Ernest Hawkins, B.D., Prebendary of St. Paul's. *Second and cheaper Edition, revised and enlarged,* Fcap. 8vo., cloth limp, red edges, 2s. 6d.

Family Prayers : — containing Psalms, Lessons, and Prayers, for
every Morning and Evening in the Week. By the Rev. Ernest Hawkins, B.D., Prebendary of St. Paul's. *Eighth Edition.* Fcap. 8vo. 1s.; sewed, 9d.

Household Prayers on Scriptural Subjects, for Four Weeks.
With Forms for various occasions. By a Member of the Church of England. *Second Edition, enlarged.* 8vo. 4s. 6d.

Forms of Prayer adapted to each Day of the Week. For use
in Families or Households. By the Rev. John Jebb, D.D., 8vo. 2s. 6d.

Walton's Lives of Donne, Wotton, Hooker, Herbert, and San-
derson. A New Edition, to which is now added a Memoir of Mr. Isaac Walton, by William Dowling, Esq. of the Inner Temple, Barrister-at-Law. With Illustrative Notes. numerous Portraits, and other Engravings, Index, &c. Crown 8vo. 10s. 6d. Calf antique, 15s. Morocco, 18s

The Life of Martin Luther. By H. Worsley, M. A., Rector of
Easton, Suffolk. 2 vols. 8vo. 1l. 4s.

Civilization considered as a Science in Relation to its Essence, its
Elements, and its End. By George Harris, F.S.A., of the Middle Temple, Barrister at Law, Author of " The Life of Lord Chancellor Hardwicke." 8vo. 12s.

The Church Hymnal, (with or without Psalms.) 12mo. Large
Type, 1s. 6d. 18mo. 1s. 32mo. for Parochial Schools, 6d.
This book is now in use in every English Diocese, and is the *Authorized*
Book in some of the Colonial Dioceses.

Three Lectures on Archbishop Cranmer. By the Rev. C. J.
Burton, M.A., Chancellor of Carlisle. 12mo. 3s.

Church Reading: according to the method advised by Thomas
Sheridan. By the Rev. J. J. Halcombe, M.A. 8vo. 3s. 6d.

The Kafir, the Hottentot, and the Frontier Farmer. Passages
of Missionary Life from the Journals of the Ven. Archdeacon Merriman.
Illustrated. Fcap. 8vo. 3s. 6d.

Lectures on the Tinnevelly Missions. By the Rev. Dr. Caldwell,
of Edeyenkoody. Crown 8vo. 2s. 6d.

The " Cruise of the Beacon." A Narrative of a Visit to the
Islands in Bass's Straits. By the Right Rev. the Bishop of Tasmania.
With Illustrations. Crown 8vo. 5s.
₊ Messrs. Bell and Daldy are agents for all the other Publications of
the Society for the Propagation of the Gospel in Foreign Parts.

The Sweet Psalmist of Israel; or, the Life of David, King of
Israel; illustrated by his own Psalms, newly versified in various metres.
By the Rev. William Shepherd, B.D. Fcap. 8vo. 5s.

Giles Witherne; or, The Reward of Disobedience. A Village
Tale for the Young. By the Rev. J. P. Parkinson, D.C.L. *Sixth
Edition.* 6d.

The Disorderly Family; or, the Village of R * * * *. A Tale for
Young Persons. In Two Parts. By a Father. 6d.; Cloth, gilt edges, 1s.

By the Rev. J. Erskine Clarke, *of Derby*.

HEART Music, for the Hearth-Ring; the Street-Walk;
the Country Stroll; the Work-Hours; the Rest-Day; the
Trouble-Time. *New Edition.* 1s. paper; 1s. 6d. cloth limp.

The Giant's Arrows. A Book for the Children of
Working People. 16mo. 6d.; cloth, 1s.

Children at Church. Twelve Simple Sermons. 2 vols. 1s. each;
1s. 6d. cloth, gilt; or together in 1 vol. cloth gilt, 2s. 6d.

Little Lectures for Little Folk. 16mo. 1s.

Plain Papers on the Social Economy of the People. Fcap. 8vo.
2s. 6d.
No. 1. Recreations of the People.—No. 2. Penny Banks.—No. 3. La-
bourers' Clubs and Working Men's Refreshment Rooms.—No. 4. Children
of the People. 6d. each.

The Devotional Library.

Edited by the Very Rev. W. F. Hook, D.D., Dean of Chichester.

A Series of Works, original or selected from well-known Church of England Divines, published at the lowest price, and suitable, from their practical character and cheapness, for Parochial distribution.

HORT Meditations for Every Day in the Year. 2 vols. (1260 pages,) 32mo. Cloth, 5s.; calf, gilt edges, 9s. Calf antique, 12s.

In Separate Parts.

ADVENT to LENT, cloth. 1s.; limp calf, gilt edges, 2s. 6d.; LENT, cloth, 9d. : calf. 2s. 3d. EASTER, cloth, 9d.; calf, 2s. 3d. TRINITY, Part I. 1s.; calf, 2s. 6d. TRINITY, Part II. 1s.; calf, 2s. 6d.

* Large Paper Edition, 4 vols. fcap. 8vo. large type. 14s. Morocco, 30s.

The Christian taught by the Church's Services. (490 pages), royal 32mo. Cloth, 2s. 6d.; calf, gilt edges, 4s. 6d. Calf antique, 6s.

In Separate Parts.

ADVENT TO TRINITY, cloth, 1s.; limp calf, gilt edges, 2s. 6d. TRINITY, cloth, 8d.; calf, 2s. 2d. MINOR FESTIVALS, 8d.; calf, 2s. 2d.

* Large Paper Edition, Fcap. 8vo. large type. 6s. 6d. Calf antique, or morocco, 11s. 6d.

Devotions for Domestic Use. 32mo. cloth, 2s.; calf, gilt edges, 4s. Calf antique, 5s. 6d. Containing:—

> The Common Prayer Book the best Companion in the Family as well as in the Temple. 3d.
> Litanies for Domestic Use, 2d.
> Family Prayers; or, Morning and Evening Services for every Day in the Week. By the Bishop of Salisbury; cloth, 6d.; calf, 2s.
> Bishop Hall's Sacred Aphorisms. Selected and arranged with the Texts to which they refer. By the Rev. R. B. Exton, M.A.; cloth, 9d.

* These are arranged together as being suitable for Domestic Use; but they may be had separately at the prices affixed.

Aids to a Holy Life. First Series. 32mo. Cloth, 1s. 6d.; calf, gilt edges, 3s. 6d. Calf antique, 5s. Containing:—

> Prayers for the Young. By Dr. Hook, ½d.
> Pastoral Address to a Young Communicant. By Dr. Hook, ½d.
> Helps to Self-Examination. By W. F. Hook, D.D., ½d.
> Directions for Spending One Day Well. By Archbishop Synge, ½d.
> Rules for the Conduct of Human Life. By Archbishop Synge. 1d.
> The Sum of Christianity, wherein a short and plain Account is given of the Christian Faith; Christian's Duty; Christian Prayer; Christian Sacrament. By C. Ellis, 1d.
> Ejaculatory Prayer; or, the Duty of Offering up Short Prayers to God on all Occasions. By R. Cook. 2d.
> Prayers for a Week. From J. Sorocold, 2d.
> Companion to the Altar; being Prayers, Thanksgivings, and Meditations. Edited by Dr. Hook. Cloth, 6d.

* Any of the above may be had for distribution at the prices affixed; they are arranged together as being suitable for Young Persons and for Private Devotion.

The Devotional Library continued.

Aids to a Holy Life. Second Series. 32mo. Cloth, 2s.; calf, gilt edges, 4s. Calf antique, 5s. 6d. Containing:—
Holy Thoughts and Prayers, arranged for Daily Use on each Day in the Week, 3d.
The Retired Christian exercised on Divine Thoughts and Heavenly Meditations. By Bishop Ken. 3d.
Penitential Reflections for the Holy Season of Lent, and other Days of Fasting and Abstinence during the Year. 6d.
The Crucified Jesus; a Devotional Commentary on the XXII and XXIII Chapters of St. Luke. By A. Horneck, D.D. 3d.
Short Reflections for every Morning and Evening during the Week. By N. Spinckes, 2d.
The Sick Man Visited; or, Meditations and Prayers for the Sick Room. By N. Spinckes, 3d.
*** These are arranged together as being suitable for Private Meditation and Prayer: they may be had separately at the prices affixed.

Helps to Daily Devotion. 32mo. Cloth, 8d. Containing:—
The Sum of Christianity, 1d.
Directions for spending One Day Well, ½d.
Helps to Self-Examination, ½d.
Short Reflections for Morning and Evening, 2d.
Prayers for a Week, 2d.

The History of our Lord and Saviour Jesus Christ; in Three Parts, with suitable Meditations and Prayers. By W. Reading, M.A. 32mo. Cloth, 2s.; calf, gilt edges, 4s. Calf antique, 5s. 6d.

Hall's Sacred Aphorisms. Selected and arranged with the Texts to which they refer, by the Rev. R. B. Exton, M.A. 32mo. cloth, 9d.; limp calf, gilt edges, 2s. 3d.

Devout Musings on the Book of Psalms. 2 vols. 32mo. Cloth, 5s.; calf, gilt edges, 9s.; calf antique, 12s. Or, in four parts, price 1s. each; limp calf, gilt edges, 2s. 6d.

The Church Sunday School Hymn Book. 32mo. cloth, 8d.; calf, gilt edges, 2s. 6d.
*** A *Large Paper Edition* for Prizes, &c. 1s. 6d.; calf, gilt edges, 3s. 6d.

HORT Meditations for Every Day in the Year. Edited by the Very Rev. W. F. Hook, D.D. *New Edition.* 4 vols. fcap. 8vo., large type, 14s.; morocco, 30s.

The Christian taught by the Church's Services. Edited by the Very Rev. W. F. Hook, D.D. *New Edition,* fcap. 8vo. large type, 6s. 6d. Antique calf, or morocco, 11s. 6d.

Holy Thoughts and Prayers, arranged for Daily Use on each Day of the Week, according to the stated Hours of Prayer. *Fifth Edition,* with additions. 16mo. Cloth, red edges, 2s.; calf, gilt edges, 3s.

A Companion to the Altar. Being Prayers, Thanksgivings, and Meditations, and the Office of the Holy Communion. Edited by the Very Rev. W. F. Hook, D.D. *Second Edition.* Handsomely printed in red and black. 32mo. Cloth, red edges, 2s. Morocco, 3s. 6d.

The Church Sunday School Hymn Book. Edited by W. F. Hook, D.D. *Large paper.* Cloth, 1s. 6d.; calf, gilt edges, 3s. 6d.
*** For cheap editions of the above Five Books, see List of the Devotional Library.

EDUCATIONAL BOOKS.

Bibliotheca Classica.

A Series of Greek and Latin Authors. With English Notes. 8vo. Edited by various Scholars, under the direction of G. Long, Esq., M.A., Classical Lecturer of Brighton College: and the late Rev. A. J. Macleane, |M.A., Head Master of King Edward's School, Bath.

ESCHYLUS. By F. A. Paley, M.A. 18*s.*

Cicero's Orations. Edited by G. Long, M.A. 4 vols. Vol. I. 16*s.*; Vol. II. 14*s*; Vol. III. 16*s.*; Vol. IV. 18*s.*

Demosthenes. By R. Whiston, M.A., Head Master of Rochester Grammar School. Vol. I. 16*s.* Vol. II. *preparing.*

Euripides. By F. A. Paley, M.A. 3 vols. 16*s.* each.

Herodotus. By J. W. Blakesley, B.D., late Fellow and Tutor of Trinity College, Cambridge. 2 vols. 32*s.*

Hesiod. By F. A. Paley, M.A. 10*s.* 6*d.*

Horace. By A. J. Macleane, M.A. 18*s.*

Juvenal and Persius. By A. J. Macleane, M.A. 14*s.*

Sophocles. By F. H. Blaydes, M.A. Vol. I. 18*s.* Vol. II. *preparing.*

Terence. By E. St. J. Parry, M.A., Balliol College, Oxford. 18*s.*

Virgil. By J. Conington, M.A., Professor of Latin at Oxford. Vol. I. containing the Bucolics and Georgics. 12*s.* Vol. II. *in the press.*

Plato. By W. H. Thompson, M.A. Vol. I.   [*Preparing.*

Grammar-School Classics.

A Series of Greek and Latin Authors. Newly Edited, with English Notes for Schools. Fcap. 8vo.

CAESARIS Commentarii de Bello Gallico. *Second Edition.* By G. Long, M.A. 5*s.* 6*d.*

Caesar de Bello Gallico, Books 1 to 3. With English Notes for Junior Classes. By G. Long, M.A. 2*s.* 6*d.*

M. Tullii Ciceronis Cato Major, Sive de Senectute, Laelius, Sive de Amicitia, et Epistolae Selectae. By G. Long, M.A. 4*s.* 6*d.*

Quinti Horatii Flacci Opera Omnia. By A. J. Macleane, 6*s.* 6*d.*

Juvenalis Satirae XVI. By H. Prior, M.A. (Expurgated Edition). 4*s.* 6*d.*

Grammar-School Classics continued.

P. Ovidii Nasonis Fastorum Libri Sex. By F. A. Paley. 5s.

C. Sallustii Crispi Catilina et Jugurtha. By G. Long, M.A. 5s.

Taciti Germania et Agricola. By P. Frost, M.A. 3s. 6d.

Xenophontis Anabasis, with Introduction; Geographical and other Notes, Itinerary, and Three Maps compiled from recent surveys. By J. F. Macmichael, B.A. *New Edition.* 5s.

Xenophontis Cyropaedia. By G. M. Gorham, M.A., late Fellow of Trinity College, Cambridge. 6s.

Uniform with the above.

The New Testament in Greek. With English Notes and Prefaces by J. F. Macmichael, B.A. 730 pages. 7s. 6d.

Cambridge Greek and Latin Texts.

THIS series is intended to supply for the use of Schools and Students cheap and accurate editions of the Classics, which shall be superior in mechanical execution to the small German editions now current in this country, and more convenient in form.

The texts of the *Bibliotheca Classica* and *Grammar School Classics*, so far as they have been published, will be adopted. These editions have taken their place amongst scholars as valuable contributions to the Classical Literature of this country, and are admitted to be good examples of the judicious and practical nature of English scholarship; and as the editors have formed their texts from a careful examination of the best editions extant, it is believed that no texts better for general use can be found.

The volumes will be well printed at the Cambridge University Press, in a 16mo. size, and will be issued at short intervals.

ÆSCHYLUS, ex novissima recensione F. A. Paley. 3s.

Cæsar de Bello Gallico, recensuit G. Long, A.M. 2s.

Cicero de Senectute et de Amicitia et Epistolæ Selectæ, recensuit G. Long, A.M. 1s. 6d.

Euripides, ex recensione F. A. Paley, A. M. 3 vols. 3s. 6d. each.

Herodotus, recensuit J. W. Blakesley, S.T.B. 2 vols. 7s.

Horatius, ex recensione A. J. Macleane, A.M. 2s. 6d.

Lucretius, recognovit H. A. J. Munro, A.M. 2s. 6d.

Sallusti Crispi Catilina et Jugurtha, recognovit G. Long, A.M. 1s. 6d.

Thucydides, recensuit J. G. Donaldson, S.T.P. 2 vols. 7s.

Vergilius, ex recensione J. Conington, A.M. 3s. 6d.

Xenophontis Anabasis recensuit J. F. Macmichael, A.B. 2s. 6d.

Novum Testamentum Graecum Textus Stephanici, 1550. Accedunt variae Lectiones editionum Bezae, Elzeviri, Lachmanni, Tischendorfii, Tregellesii, curante F. H. Scrivener, A.M. 4s. 6d.

Also, on 4to. writing paper, for MSS. notes. Half bound, gilt top, 21s.

ffortign Classics.

With English Notes for Schools. Uniform with the GRAMMAR SCHOOL
CLASSICS. Fcap. 8vo.

VENTURES de Télémaque, par Fénelon. Edited by
C. J. Delille. *Second Edition, revised.* 4s. 6d.

Histoire de Charles XII. par Voltaire. Edited by
L. Direy. *Second Edition, revised.* 3s. 6d.

Select Fables of La Fontaine. *Third Edition, revised.* Edited by
F. Gasc, M.A. 3s.

" None need now be afraid to introduce this eminently French author,
either on account of the difficulty of translating him, or the occasional
licence of thought and expression in which he indulges. The renderings
of idiomatic passages are unusually good, and the purity of English perfect."—*Athenæum.*

Picciola, by X. B. Saintine. Edited by Dr. Dubuc. 3s. 6d.

This interesting story has been selected with the intention of providing
for schools and young persons a good specimen of contemporary French
literature, free from the solecisms which are frequently met with in writers
of a past age.

Schiller's Wallenstein, complete Text. With Notes, &c. by Dr.
A. Buchheim. 6s 6d.

Classical Tables. 8vo.

OTABILIA Quædam : or, the principal tenses of such
Irregular Greek Verbs and such elementary Greek, Latin,
and French Constructions as are of constant occurrence. 1s. 6d.

Greek Accidence. By the Rev. P. Frost, M.A. 1s.

Latin Accidence. By the Rev. P. Frost, M. A. 1s.

Latin Versification. 1s.

The Principles of Latin Syntax. 1s.

Homeric Dialect: its leading Forms and Peculiarities. By J. S.
Baird, T.C.D. 1s. 6d.

A Catalogue of Greek Verbs, Irregular and Defective; their
leading formations, tenses in use, and dialectic inflexions; with a copious
Appendix, containing Paradigms for conjugation, Rules for formation of
tenses, &c. &c. By J. S. Baird, T.C.D. *New Edition, revised.* 3s. 6d.

Richmond Rules to form the Ovidian Distich, &c. By J. Tate,
M.A. *New Edition, revised.* 1s. 6d.

N Atlas of Classical Geography, containing 24 Maps;
constructed by W. Hughes, and edited by G. Long. *New Edition,* with coloured outlines, and an Index of Places. 12s. 6d.

A Grammar School Atlas of Classical Geography. The
Maps constructed by W. Hughes, and edited by G. Long. Imp. 8vo. 5s.

First Classical Maps, with Chronological Tables of Grecian and
Roman History, Tables of Jewish Chronology, and a Map of Palestine.
By the Rev. J. Tate, M.A. *Third Edition.* Imp. 8vo. 7s. 6d.

The Choephorae of Æschylus and its Scholia. Revised and interpreted by J. F. Davies, Esq., B.A., Trin. Coll., Dublin. 8vo. 7s. 6d.

Homer and English Metre. An Essay on the Translating of the Iliad and Odyssey. With a Literal Rendering in the Spenserian Stanza of the First Book of the Odyssey, and Specimens of the Iliad. William G. T. Barter, Esq., Author of "A Literal Translation, in Spenserian Stanza, of the Iliad of Homer." Crown 8vo. 6s. 6d.

Auxilia Graeca: containing Forms of Parsing and Greek Trees, the Greek Prepositions, Rules of Accentuation, Greek Idioms, &c. &c. By the Rev. H. Fowler, M.A. 12mo. 3s. 6d.

A Latin Grammar. By T. Hewitt Key, M.A., F.R S., Professor of Comparative Grammar, and Head Master of the Junior School, in University College. *Third Edition, revised.* Post 8vo. 8s.

A Short Latin Grammar, for Schools. By T. H. Key, M.A., F.R.S. *Third Edition.* Post 8vo. 3s. 6d.

Latin Accidence. Consisting of the Forms, and intended to prepare boys for Key's Short Latin Grammar. Post 8vo. 2s.

A First Cheque Book for Latin Verse Makers. By the Rev. F. Gretton, Stamford Free Grammar School. 1s. 6d. Key, 2s. 6d.

Reddenda; or Passages with Parallel Hints for translation into Latin Prose and Verse. By the Rev. F. E. Gretton. Crown 8vo. 4s. 6d.

Rules for the Genders of Latin Nouns, and the Perfects and Supines of Verbs; with hints on Construing, &c. By H. Haines, M.A. 1s. 6d.

Latin Prose Lessons. By the Rev. A. Church, M.A., one of the Masters of Merchant Taylors' School. Fcap. 8vo. 2s. 6d.

Materials for Latin Prose Composition. By the Rev. P. Frost, M.A., St. John's College, Cambridge. *Second Edition.* 12mo. 2s. 6d. Key, 4s.

The Works of Virgil, closely rendered into English Rhythm, and illustrated from British Poets of the 16th, 17th, and 18th Centuries. By the Rev. R. C. Singleton, M.A. 2 vols. post 8vo. 18s.

Quintus Horatius Flaccus. Illustrated with 50 Engravings from the Antique. Fcap. 8vo. 5s. Morocco, 9s.

Selections from Ovid: Amores, Tristia, Heroides, Metamorphoses. With English Notes, by the Rev. A. J. Macleane, M.A. Fcap. 8vo. 3s. 6d.

Sabrinae Corolla in hortulis Regiae Scholae Salopiensis contexuerunt tres viri floribus legendis. *Editio Altera.* 8vo. 12s. Morocco, 21s.

Rudimentary Art Instruction for Artisans and others, and for Schools. FREEHAND OUTLINE. Part I. OUTLINE FROM OUTLINE, or from the Flat. 3s. Part II. OUTLINE FROM OBJECTS, or from the Round. 4s. By John Bell, Sculptor. Oblong 4to.

A Graduated Series of Exercises in Elementary Algebra, with an Appendix containing Papers of Miscellaneous Examples. Designed for the Use of Schools. By the Rev. G. F. Wright, M.A., Mathematical Master at Wellington College. Crown 8vo. 3s. 6d.

The Elements of Euclid. Books I.—VI. XI. 1—21; XII. 1, 2; a new text, based on that of Simson, with Exercises. Edited by H. J Hose, late Mathematical Master of Westminster School. Fcap. 4s. 6d.

A **Graduated Series of Exercises on the Elements of Euclid:** Books I.—VI.; XI. 1—21; XII. 1, 2. Selected and arranged by Henry J. Hose, M.A. 12mo. 1*s.*

The Enunciations and Figures belonging to the Propositions in the First Six and part of the Eleventh Books of Euclid's Elements, (usually read in the Universities,) prepared for Students in Geometry By the Rev. J. Brasse, D.D. *New Edition.* Fcap. 8vo. 1*s.* On cards, in case, 5*s.* 6*d.*; without the Figures, 6*d.*

A **Compendium of Facts and Formulæ in Pure and Mixed** Mathematics. For the use of Mathematical Students. By G. R. Smalley, B.A., F.R.A.S. Fcap. 8vo. 3*s.* 6*d.*

A **Table of Anti-Logarithms; containing to seven places of deci-**mals, natural numbers, answering to all Logarithms from ·00001 to ·99999; and an improved table of Gauss' Logarithms, by which may be found the Logarithm of the sum or difference of two quantities. With an Appendix, containing a Table of Annuities for three Joint Lives at 3 per cent. Carlisle. By H. E. Filipowski. *Third Edition.* 8vo. 15*s.*

Handbook of the Slide Rule: showing its applicability to Arith-metic, including Interest and Annuities; Mensuration, including Land. Surveying. With numerous Examples and useful Tables. By W. H. Bayley, H. M. East India Civil Service. 12mo. 6*s.*

The Mechanics of Construction; including the Theories on the Strength of Materials, Roofs, Arches, and Suspension Bridges. With numerous Examples. By Stephen Fenwick, Esq., of the Royal Military Academy, Woolwich. 8vo. 12*s.*

A NEW FRENCH COURSE, BY MONS. F. E. A. GASC, M.A.
French Master at Brighton College.

E Petit Compagnon: a French Talk-book for Little Children. With 52 Illustrations. 16mo. 2*s.* 6*d.*

First French Book; being a New, Practical, and Easy Method of Learning the Elements of the French Language. *New Edition.* Fcap. 8vo. 1*s.* 6*d.*

French Fables, for Beginners, in Prose, with an Index of all the words at the end of the work. Fcap. 8vo. 2*s.*

Second French Book; being a Grammar and Exercise Book, on a new and practical plan, exhibiting the chief peculiarities of the French Language, as compared with the English, and intended as a sequel to the "First French Book." Fcap. 8vo. 2*s.* 6*d.*

A **Key to the First and Second French Books.** Fcap. 8vo. 3*s.* 6*d.*

Histoires Amusantes et Instructives; or, Selections of Complete Stories from the best French Authors, who have written for the Young. With English Notes. *New Edition.* Fcap. 8vo. 2*s.* 6*d.*

Practical Guide to Modern French Conversation: containing:— I. The most current and useful Phrases in Every-Day Talk; II. Everybody's Necessary Questions and Answers in Travel-Talk. Fcap. 2*s.* 6*d.*

French Poetry for the Young. With English Notes, and preceded by a few plain Rules of French Prosody. Fcap. 8vo. 2*s.*

Materials for French Prose Composition; or, Selections from the best English Prose Writers. With copious Foot Notes, and Hints for Idiomatic Renderings. *New Edition.* Fcap. 8vo. 4*s.* 6*d.* Key, 6*s.*

HE French Drama; being a Selection of the best Tragedies and Comedies of Molière, Racine, P. Corneille, T. Corneille, and Voltaire. With Arguments in English at the head of each scene, and Notes, Critical and Explanatory, by A. Gombert. 18mo. Sold separately at 1s. each. Half-bound, 1s. 6d. each.

COMEDIES BY MOLIERE.

Le Misanthrope.
L'Avare.
Le Bourgeois Gentilhomme.
Le Tartuffe.
Le Malade Imaginaire.
Les Femmes Savantes.
Les Fourberies de Scapin.

Les Précieuses Ridicules.
. L'Ecole des Femmes.
L'Ecole des Maris.
Le Médecin Malgré Lui.
M. de Pourceaugnac.
Amphitryon.

TRAGEDIES, &c. BY RACINE.

La Thébaïde, ou les Frères
  Ennemis.
Alexandre le Grand.
Andromaque.
Les Plaideurs, (Com.)
Britannicus.
Bérénice.

Bajazet.
Mithridate.
Iphigénie.
Phédre.
Esther.
Athalie.

TRAGEDIES, &c. BY P. CORNEILLE.

Le Cid.
Horace.
Cinna.
Polyeucte.

Pompée.

BY T. CORNEILLE.

Ariane.

PLAYS BY VOLTAIRE.

Brutus.
Zaire.
Alzire.
Orestes.

Le Fanatisme.
Mérope.
La Mort de César.
Semiramis.

Le Nouveau Trésor: or, French Student's Companion: designed to facilitate the Translation of English into French at Sight. *Thirteenth Edition*, with Additions. By M. E*** S*****. 12mo. Roan, 3s. 6d.

A Test-Book for Students: Examination Papers for Students preparing for the Universities or for Appointments in the Army and Civil Service, and arranged for General Use in Schools. By the Rev. Thomas Stantial, M.A., Head Master of the Grammar School, Bridgwater. Part I.—History and Geography. 2s. 6d. Part II.—Language and Literature. 2s. 6d. Part III.—Mathematical Science. 2s. 6d. Part IV.—Physical Science. 1s. 6d. Or in 1 vol., Crown 8vo., 7s. 6d.

Tables of Comparative Chronology, illustrating the division of Universal History into Ancient, Mediæval, and Modern History; and containing a System of Combinations, distinguished by a particular type, to assist the Memory in retaining Dates. By W. E. Bickmore and the Rev. C. Bickmore, M.A. *Third Edition.* 4to. 5s.

A Course of Historical and Chronological Instruction. By W. E. Bickmore. 2 Parts. 12mo. 3s. 6d. each.

A Practical Synopsis of English History: or, A General Summary of Dates and Events for the use of Schools, and Candidates for Public Examinations. By Arthur Bowes. *Third Edition*, enlarged. 8vo. 2s.

The Student's Text-Book of English and General History, from
B. C. 100 to the present time. With Genealogical Tables, and a Sketch
of the English Constitution. By D. Beale. *Sixth Edition.* Post 8vo.
Sewed, 2s. Cloth, 2s. 6d.
" This is very much in advance of most works we have seen devoted to
similar purposes. We can award very high praise to a volume which
may prove invaluable to teachers and taught."—*Athenæum.*

The Elements of the English Language for Schools and Colleges.
By Ernest Adams, Ph. D. University College School. *New Edition, enlarged, and improved.* Crown 8vo. 4s. 6d. [*Ready.*

The Geographical Text-Book; a Practical Geography, calculated
to facilitate the study of that useful science, by a constant reference to
the Blank Maps. By M. E ... S ..... 12mo. 2s.
II. The Blank Maps done up separately. 4to. 2s. coloured.

The 1862 Edition of Under Government: an Official Key to the
Civil Service, and Guide for Candidates seeking Appointments under the
Crown. By J. C. Parkinson, Inland Revenue, Somerset House. *New
Edition.* Cr. 8vo. 3s. 6d.

Government Examinations; being a Companion to " Under
Government," and a Guide to the Civil Service Examinations. By J. C.
Parkinson. Crown 8vo. 2s. 6d.

The Manual of Book-keeping ; by an Experienced Clerk. 12mo.
Eighth Edition. 4s.

Double Entry Elucidated. By B. W. Foster. 4to. 8s. 6d.

Penmanship, Theoretical and Practical, Illustrated and Explained
By B. F. Foster. 12mo. *New Edition.* 2s. 6d.

Goldsmith's (J.) Copy Books: five sorts, large, text, round, small,
and mixed. Post 4to. on fine paper. 6s. per dozen.

The Young Ladies' School Record: or, Register of Studies and
conduct. 12mo. 6d.

Welchman on the Thirty-nine Articles of the Church of England,
with Scriptural Proofs, &c. 18mo. 2s. or interleaved for Students, 3s.

Bishop Jewel's Apology for the Church of England, with his
famous Epistle on the Council of Trent, and a Memoir. 32mo. 2s.

A Short Explanation of the Epistles and Gospels of the Christian
Year, with Questions for Schools. Royal 32mo. 2s. 6d.; calf, 4s. 6d.

Manual of Astronomy : a Popular Treatise on Descriptive, Physical, and Practical Astronomy. By John Drew, F.R.A.S. *Second Edition.* Fcap. 8vo. 5s.

The First Book of Botany. Being a Plain and Brief Introduction
to that Science for Schools and Young Persons. By Mrs. Loudon. Illustrated with 36 Wood Engravings. *Second Edition.* 18mo. 1s.

English Poetry for Classical Schools; or, Florilegium Poeticum
Anglicanum. 12mo. 1s. 6d.

BELL AND DALDY'S ILLUSTRATED SCHOOL BOOKS.
Royal 16mo.

CHOOL Primer. 6*d.*

School Reader. 1*s.*   [*Shortly.*

Poetry Book for Schools. 1*s.*

COURSE OF INSTRUCTION FOR THE YOUNG, BY HORACE
GRANT.

XERCISES for the Improvement of the Senses ; for
Young Childdren. 18mo. 1*s.* 6*d.*

Geography for Young Children. *New Edition.* 18mo. 2*s.*

Arithmetic for Young Children. *New Edition.* 18mo. 1*s.* 6*d.*

Arithmetic. Second Stage. *New Edition.* 18mo. 3*s.*

PERIODICALS.

OTES and Queries: a Medium of Intercommunication
for Literary Men, Artists, Antiquaries, Genealogists, &c.
Published every Saturday. 4to. 4*d.,* stamped, 5*d.*
Vols. I. to XII. Second Series now ready, 10*s.* 6*d.* each.
⁎ General Index to the First Series, 5*s.*
———————————— Second Series.   [*Preparing.*

The Monthly Medley for Happy Homes. A New Miscellany
for Children. Conducted by the Rev. J. Erskine Clarke. Price 1*d.*
Volumes for 1860 and 1861, 1*s.* 6*d.* each.

The Parish Magazine. Edited by J. Erskine Clarke, M.A.,
Derby. Monthly, price 1*d.* Volumes for 1859, 1860, and 1861, 1*s.* 6*d.* and
2*s.* each.

The Mission Field : a Monthly Record of the Proceedings of the
Society for the Propagation of the Gospel. Vols. II. to VI. post 8vo. 3*s.*
each. (Vol. I. is out of print.) Continued in Numbers, 2*d.* each.

The Gospel Missionary. Published for the Society for the Propagation of the Gospel in Foreign Parts, Monthly at ½*d.* Vols. II. to
XI. in cloth, 1*s.* each. (Vol. I. is out of print.)

Missions to the Heathen ; being Records of the Progress of the
Efforts made by the Society for the Propagation of the Gospel in Foreign
Parts for the Conversion of the Heathen. Published occasionally in a
cheap form for distribution, at prices varying from 1*d.* to 1*s.* 6*d.* each.
Nos. 1 to 43 are already published.

Church in the Colonies, consisting chiefly of Journals by the
Colonial Bishops of their Progress and Special Visitations. Published
occasionally at prices varying from 2*d.* to 1*s.* 6*d.* each. Nos. 1 to 37 are
already published.

CLARKE'S COMMERCIAL COPY - BOOKS.
Price 4*d.* A liberal allowance to Schools and Colleges.

The FIRST COPY-BOOK contains *elementary turns*, with a broad mark like a T, which divides a well-formed turn into two equal parts. This exercise enables the learner to judge of *form, distance, and proportion.*

The SECOND contains *large-hand letters*, and the means by which such letters may be properly combined ; the joinings in writing being probably as difficult to learn as the form of each character. This book also gives the whole alphabet, not in separate letters, but rather as one *word ;* and, at the end of the alphabet, the difficult letters are repeated so as to render the writing of the pupil more thorough and *uniform.*

The THIRD contains additional *large-hand practice.*

The FOURTH contains *large-hand words*, commencing with *unflourished* capitals; and the words being short, the capitals in question receive the attention they demand. As Large, and Extra Large-text, to which the fingers of the learner are not equal, have been dispensed with in this series, the popular objection of having *too many Copy-books* for the pupil to drudge through, is now fairly met. When letters are very large, the scholar cannot compass them without stopping to change the position of his hand, which *destroys* the *freedom* which such writing is intended to promote.

The FIFTH contains the essentials of a useful kind of *small-hand.* There are first, as in large-hand, five easy letters of the alphabet, forming four copies, which of course are repeated. Then follows the remainder of the alphabet, with the difficult characters alluded to. The letters in this hand, especially the *a, c, d, g, o,* and *q*, are so formed that when the learner will have to correspond, his writing will not appear stiff. The copies in this book are not *mere Large-hand reduced.*

The SIXTH contains *small-hand copies*, with instructions as to the manner in which the pupil should hold his pen, so that when he leaves school he may not merely have some facility in copying, but really possess the information on the subject of writing which he may need at any future time.

The SEVENTH contains the foundation for a style of *small-hand*, adapted to females, *moderately pointed.*

The EIGHTH contains copies for females ; and the holding of the pen is, of course, the subject to which they specially relate.

This Series is specially adapted for those who are preparing for a commercial life. It is generally found when a boy leaves school that his writing is of such a character that it is some months before it is available for book-keeping or accounts. The special object of this Series of Copy-Books is to form his writing in such a style that he may be put to the work of a counting-house at once. By following this course from the first the writing is kept free and legible, whilst it avoids unnecessary flourishing.

Specimens of hand-writing after a short course may be seen on application to the Publishers.

. BELL AND DALDY'S

POCKET VOLUMES.

A SERIES OF SELECT WORKS OF
FAVOURITE AUTHORS.

THE intention of the Publishers is to produce a Series of Volumes adapted for general reading, moderate in price, compact and elegant in form, and executed in a style fitting them to be permanently preserved.

They do not profess to compete with the so-called cheap volumes. They believe that a cheapness which is attained by the use of inferior type and paper, and absence of editorial care, and which results in volumes that no one cares to keep, is a false cheapness. They desire rather to produce books superior in quality, and relatively as cheap.

Each volume will be carefully revised by a competent editor, and printed at the Chiswick Press, on fine paper, with new type and ornaments and initial letters specially designed for the series.

The *Pocket Volumes* will include all classes of Literature, both copyright and non-copyright ;—Biography, History, Voyages, Travels, Poetry, sacred and secular, Books of Adventure and Fiction. They will include Translations of Foreign Books, and also such American Literature as may be considered worthy of adoption.

The Publishers desire to respect the moral claims of authors who cannot secure legal copyright in this country, and to remunerate equitably those whose works they may reprint.

The books will be issued at short intervals, in paper covers, at various prices, from 1*s.* to 3*s.* 6*d.*, and in cloth, top edge gilt, at 6*d.* per volume extra, in half morocco, Roxburgh style, at 1*s.* extra, in antique or best plain morocco (Hayday), at 4*s.* extra.

Now Ready.	*Preparing.*
The Robin Hood Ballads. 2*s.* 6*d.*	White's Natural History of Selborne.
The Midshipman. By Capt. Basil Hall, R.N. 3*s.*	Coleridge's Poems.
	The Conquest of India. By Capt. Basil Hall, R.N.
The Lieutenant and Commander. By the same Author. 3*s.*	Sea Songs and Ballads. By Charles Dibdin, and others.
Southey's Life of Nelson. 2*s.* 6*d.*	Walton's Lives of Donne, Wotton, Hooker, &c.
George Herbert's Poems. 2*s.*	Walton's Complete Angler.
George Herbert's Works. 3*s.*	Gray's Poems.
Longfellow's Poems. 2*s.* 6*d.*	Goldsmith's Poems.
Lamb's Tales from Shakspeare. 2*s.* 6*d.*	Goldsmith's Vicar of Wakefield.
Milton's Paradise Lost. 2*s.* 6*d.*	Henry Vaughan's Poems.
Milton's Paradise Regained and other Poems. 2*s.* 6*d.*	Burns's Poems.
	Burns's Songs.
	And others.

CHISWICK PRESS :—PRINTED BY WHITTINGHAM AND WILKINS,
TOOKS COURT, CHANCERY LANE.